4.95

Echoes FROM THE Past

JUNE MASTERS BACHER

HARVEST HOUSE PUBLISHERS
Eugene, OR 97402

Other Books by June Masters Bacher:

Love is a Gentle Stranger
Love's Silent Song
Diary of a Loving Heart
Love Leads Home
Journey to Love
Dreams Beyond Tomorrow
The Heart That Lingers
Until There Was You
When Love Shines Through
With All My Heart
A Mother's Joy
Kitchen Delights
Quiet Moments for Women

Scripture quotations are from the King James Version of the Bible.

ECHOES FROM THE PAST

Copyright © 1985 by Harvest House Publishers
Eugene, Oregon 97402

ISBN 0-89081-461-9

Printed in the United States of America.

To
my "family" at Harvest House
whose patience and encouragement
have inspired me
through the years!

Echoes from the Past

Honour thy father and mother, which is the first commandment with promise, that it may be well with thee, and thou mayest live long on the earth.

—Ephesians 6:2,3

Faith, like light, should always be simple and unbending; while *love*, like warmth, should beam forth on every side, and bend to every necessity of life!

—Martin Luther

1

If Kitty Fairfield's car radio had been tuned to Tucson, the nearest city, she would have heard the storm warning. Forewarned, she would neither have invaded Clayton Madrone's life nor had Rhett Dawson invade hers. But the three-year-old station wagon was new to her. She was having a hard enough time figuring out its personality and following the ancient road map spread out on the seat between her and the mongrel German shepherd bunched in sleep beside her. This was no time to fumble with the mysterious buttons on the dashboard, one of which would

7

have put her in touch with the outside world.

Besides, frightening as the thought was, she was lost—lost in the middle of this no-man's-land called *desert*. All signs of civilization had long since been swallowed up by the dark jaws of the night.

"What are we going to do, pal?" she whispered. There was no sign that the dog heard. Newly acquired like the wagon, the animal was undoubtedly as weary as she—having wandered for days without food or water before being impounded. And now, this long, hard ride. Was early May always so hot?

Holding onto the wheel with one hand, Kitty reached with the other and massaged the stiff knots of fatigue in her neck. *What ARE we going to do?* she asked herself.

Kitty remembered from her little camping experience that the rule was to find a stream and follow it downward. Good advice in Seattle, where there were as many streams as there were saguaro cacti in this Arizona desert. Standing with their spiny arms spread out as if to defy all human intrusion, each gigantic cactus was almost identical to its neighbor. It was easy to get lost. And yet how had it happened? There was only one road. Wasn't that what the service station attendant said some five hours ago? "No houses. Nothin' but them cactus and sidewinders 'twixt here and the 'Circle Left Ranch'! How come you're goin' there all alone and all?"

How *did* she happen to be going there? Straining to see some sign of lodging somewhere ahead, Kitty let her mind wander momentarily back to the telegram. That's when it all began. It was folded away in her purse. But every word was stamped indelibly on her brain.

> AS SOLE SURVIVOR OF LAWRENCE LEE FAIRFIELD, YOU, KITTY LYNN FAIR-FIELD—HIS DAUGHTER AND ONLY HEIR—ARE HEREBY NOTIFIED OF HIS PASSING; FURTHER, HIS LAST WILL AND TESTAMENT LEAVING TO YOU HIS PARCEL OF PROPERTY. . . .

The telegram went on to give the location of "said property, hereinafter referred to as 'Circle Left Ranch' " . . . what identification to bring along . . . and suggested that should Miss Fairfield wish to dispose of "Circle Left" as opposed to appearing, she should so state in a formal letter mailed to the address given. And it bore the impressive name of Gotschalk & Partners, Attorneys-at-Law.

It all looked official enough. But Kitty was unable to believe it could be anything but a cruel joke . . . but who . . .? Why would her father, who had never bothered to try to get in touch with her during his lifetime, leave anything to her? Shouldn't the property have gone to his second wife? Her own mother had said that Lawrence Fairfield, ever the charmer, had married a second time—an assertion that his daughter never bothered check out. And how ironic that her mother, after a lingering illness which spanned most of Kitty's 21 years—at least, those after her parents separated—should be followed in death so soon by her husband!

Kitty was in a state of deep remorse when the telegram reached her. Caring for her mother had taken all of her time. So there were no friends to whom she could turn, and no family on her

mother's side. And the same was true for her
father—unless the whole thing was a hoax.

Her first reaction was one of complete puzzlement.
A call to the number given in the telegram gave her
some answers, but not to the parts which puzzled
her most of all. Her father, the senior Mr. Gotschalk
said, had lived on the ranch all his life (Why, then,
had her mother said she had no idea where he was?)
There was no cash and the place was heavily mortgaged, not to mention the need for repairs. But it
was well worth redeeming, some 500 acres...
(Mother, who claimed to "hate being cooped up,"
had once lived on a 500-acre ranch?) How different
life might have been for them all...

The message came at a time when Kitty was
desperately wondering not where to pick up the
threads of her life but how to begin it. She had no
skills—certainly none that would be of help on a
ranch. The sensible thing to do—the *only* thing to
do—was call back and tell the lawyer to dispose of
the property as best he could, and to ask for a
photograph of her father...

Then, seized by a sudden sense of adventure—
totally foreign to her nature—Kitty's third reaction
came. She would settle up here, notify the landlady
she was vacating the small apartment, and use some
of Mother's small insurance policy to buy a second-
hand car. That would leave her enough cash to make
the trip from Washington to Arizona and see the
place for herself. It would be wonderful to have
breathing space.

In less time than seemed possible, Kitty had closed
out her existence. *Existence* was the right word,
she'd thought, as she finished packing her few
belongings into the station wagon—for one could

hardly call "living" the routine that she and Mother had. They simply went on doing what had to be done, without thinking, questioning, or feeling— just reacting, the way Grandmother Cramer had done before them.

Once on the open road, away from the squeezed-together houses, smoke, and fog of the city, Kitty had no misgivings. Instead, she was filled with anticipation for the first time in her life. *Everything will be all right*, she found herself thinking. And then, *I know where I am...I'm no stranger...This is home.* That thought had come at the edge of the desert. There was something familiar about it. But how could there be?

Impulsively she had pulled to the side of the road. The vastness was awesome, and the never-ending barrenness was a sharp contrast to the verdant forests she had left behind. Yet there was a certain mystery to the far-distant purple foothills, a certain charm to the near-cloudless sky. Ahead stood a solitary cluster of tree-size saguaro cacti, huddled together like secretive friends, and everywhere there was sunwashed sand.

"It's beckoning us. This *is* home," Kitty remembered repeating as she pulled back onto the narrow road.

But that was before night, like a heavy veil, came down to hem her in...before the clusters of cacti moved toward one another in strange alliance, their density almost impenetrable to her tired eyes... before she realized she was lost.

Shuddering now, Kitty lifted her foot from the gas pedal. Maybe the best thing to do was turn around, but the service station was miles back and she was uncertain as to whether there would be tourists' accommodations anyway. Easing the car to the shoulder, she tried to remember if she had seen a car since turning onto this road. What *could* she do?

Near tears, Kitty rested her head against the back of the seat for a moment and gazed at the black sky visible through the windshield. The great dome seemed so close above her and so crowded with brilliant clusters of stars. Maybe she could get a sense of direction from the Big Dipper. . .

It was then, without warning, that the storm struck. Overhead there was a blinding flash of lightning which seemed to shatter the sky and bring it to earth like a shower of flaming confetti. Simultaneously there was a deafening rumble of thunder. At Kitty's cry of alarm, the dog moved closer to her and ran a damp nose across her hand.

"I'm scared," Kitty whispered to the dog. Shivering, she reached over the animal's body in an effort to roll up the window. It was no use. The window was stuck—as were two of the others, though she valiantly struggled with them. All the while she was vaguely aware that a stiff wind had blown in, seemingly from the four corners of the earth, filling the air with the smell of rain. There *must* be a way to get the windows closed against the inevitable downpour!

Even if her heavy brown hair had not come unpinned to form a blind, the clouds, now laced together for a storm, would have won out. It was as if somebody had pulled a plug. The sky simply opened and the rain came down in torrents, whipping through the open windows, soaking the upholstery, and now covering the floorboard. How *could* rain fall so fast? But even as she wondered,

Kitty saw that the area around her was a solid sheet of water.

"We have to get out of here!" When Kitty spoke, the dog whined uneasily, his great body shaking.

"Calm, keep calm!" Kitty contemplated her plight aloud. "As much responsibility as I've had, surely I can handle this. We'll drive to the nearest house—find shelter—"

Her voice faltered and stopped. There were no houses! Without thinking further, she turned the key in the ignition and, with a grind of gears, lurched forward. Then the nightmare began. The wagon went into a spin, turned completely around, and nosed into the ditch—the rear bumper high in the air while the front of the vehicle pointed back in the general direction of Tucson. The dog, alarmed now, began to bark, nervously leaping back and forth between the seats as if begging her to abandon the wagon. Animals could sense danger.

And the dog was right! It was then that Kitty saw how high the water had risen around them. And with that something clicked in her exhausted brain. FLASH FLOOD AREA! Over and over she had read the signs in the long, lonely drive. Why, they could be drowned here! Somehow she managed to climb out the window and commanded the dog to follow.

The afternoon had been unbearably hot, so the earth was still warm from the molten sun. In spite of it, Kitty shivered with a cold born of fear. Rain coursed down her face, making it almost impossible to breathe. Her sodden clothes clung like a second skin. One shoe loosened and fell from her foot—and then the other. But still they did not stop—the rain-soaked girl and the enormous mongrel at her side, running, *running*, not even checking directions...

Kitty was breathing hard. Her vision was blurred. Later she had no clear memory of having spotted a light. She only knew that a door loomed before her. She knocked. There was no answer. She knocked again. Maybe she screamed. She did remember hearing the pitiful wail of the dog by her side.

When at last the door opened, it was with the deliberate calm reserved for intruders when there is a NO TRESPASSING sign posted. Her heart sank when she saw the steel-blue eyes—steady and unwavering, but cold, appraising, and indifferent.

"I—we—are in trouble. I know we're unwelcome, but—"

At that point her voice failed and worse, she fell against him. "Just what I need," he muttered. "A drowning girl!"

Navajo rugs...rows of books...soft lamplight...
and the sound of a human voice. Kitty, teetering on
the edge of consciousness, was unable at first to see
the speaker. She had only the vague feeling of having been dragged into the big, lamp-lit room—either
willingly or unwillingly.

Kitty felt a warm blackness creeping over her
body. If only she could lie down. Her eyelids were
heavy—so heavy.

"Don't sleep! Wake up!" The human voice sounded
angry. She forced her eyes open briefly and looked
into the speaker's face. High cheekbones. Black

beard. Broad shoulders. Slim waist. And an allover glow that boasted of vigor born of wholesome living. But why was he so angry, so suspicious, so afraid of being found out? He didn't like women... or didn't trust strangers...or was afraid of dogs? Dogs! Where was the dog?

"John Doe—the dog?" she whispered. And then she was drifting away again.

As the first layer of sleep hovered over her, Kitty heard her host say, "John Doe indeed!" And apparently it was the ridiculous name that caused him to laugh. It was a nice sound, low and mellow—totally unlike the aloofness in his face, and betraying an inner softness. Then she felt this man—this *stranger!*—shucking off the outer layer of her clothing and toweling her dry before covering her with a scratchy blanket. And she was helpless—too weak to fight against him. Then, just before total darkness, Kitty was sure he brushed back her drying hair and lightly planted a kiss on her forehead. "Okay, you're here—but remember, not by invitation. You look so innocent—so childlike—but I refuse to be taken in! You'll be sorry you invaded my privacy—"

Kitty judged she had slept for an hour. She felt refreshed and wide awake. She also felt she was being watched, and was relieved when she saw the great, liquid eyes of John Doe, the mongrel German shepherd, fastened on her protectively. "You and I'll be great friends," she whispered as she cast a quick look around the room. Beamed ceiling. A battered piano. Paintings along the walls. And a dreadfully untidy desk.

"Exactly where am I?" She asked herself aloud, aware for the first time that she was only half-dressed

. . .and wasn't this a man's bathrobe she had on? "Is this my destination?"

"I've no idea what your destination was, but you were blown off course!" The gruff voice she remembered was right behind her, causing her to jump and pull the robe high up under her chin.

He stepped around the couch on which she lay, his face in the shadows. "I—I—" Kitty fumbled for words. "We were on our way to the 'Circle Left.' It's a ranch—"

The man turned toward her impatiently, his blue eyes blazing again. What was it about her that annoyed him so much? She was about to ask so she could apologize when he went on speaking. "You obviously know your way around or you wouldn't be this far from civilization alone. So how on this green earth did you end up *here*—unless you planned it?"

Suddenly Kitty felt angry herself. "Where exactly is *here*?" she asked coldly. "If you will explain, I'll try and get a wrecker—"

"Wrecker!" The word was almost a moan. "What have you done, where have you come from, why are you here, and who are you?"

In spite of her embarrassment and the seriousness of the situation, Kitty giggled. After all, she was in a predicament and it was natural that he would be curious.

"What I've done, Your Honor," she said with a straight face, "is manage to get my station wagon in a ditch somewhere in this desert—I don't know where. And I came from Seattle by way of Tucson— thence to wherever the car is ditched. I am here because of my misfortune. And, as to who I am— my name is Kitty Fairfield."

For a second there was a flicker of amusement in his eyes, and the corners of his mouth turned upward ever so slightly. Then he frowned. "None of this tells me anything—which is just as well, because you aren't going to be staying!"

Well, of all the nerve! "You're right," she said as calmly as she could manage. "But at least you can offer me a cup of coffee and the use of your telephone—and I don't even know your name."

"Stop pretending!"

The two words came so unexpectedly that Kitty, having no idea what the man meant, could only stare at him in numb amazement. Sure that her silence only added up to more evidence against her, she could only watch his closely cropped beard in fascination. Every hair seemed to bristle in his anger.

Finally she found her voice. "How far am I from 'Circle Left'?" Her voice had resumed its natural childlike quality. The brief assertiveness was gone. Even Kitty was aware of the change. Mother and Grandmother had done their homework well—conditioning her to a certain passivity. That was a woman's role, they said. And Kitty had never thought to question it any more than she had questioned her father's whereabouts. "If you'll tell me how far—"

"Far enough to find me. Congratulations!"

"Thank you, Mr. Whatever-your-name is—"

"Madrone—Clayton Madrone."

Was the name supposed to mean something to her? The very idea would have been amusing if this infuriatingly rude man had known what a sheltered life she had led. How few men she knew! He must have an ego as big as all outdoors to think a total stranger from the Pacific Northwest would know his name. But wait! He had accused her of worse. The idea that she had followed him here was preposterous—so ridiculous that Kitty decided to ignore it. That would let some of the air out of his tires!

"Thank you, Mr. Madrone," she said primly. "We can skip the coffee, but may I use your telephone?"

Clayton Madrone's sigh was one of despair. "You really don't know these parts, do you? The storm was a whopper, even for here. The lines may not be repaired for days."

Kitty sucked in her breath. "Then how am I—?"

"Oh, I'll see that you get out! But I can't promise you what you came for. You're tougher than you look to have tried—"

"I have no idea what you're talking about," Kitty's voice was trembling in spite of her efforts to sound calm. She was humiliated, trapped, and frightened—and she didn't even know where her clothes were! Suddenly, with no more warning than the storm had given her, she burst into tears. Then, to her horror, great childish sobs tore through her frail body. And just as unexpectedly she was in his arms, held close against the softness of his khaki shirt—near the left pocket, she judged, as she felt a writing pen against her ear and heard the pounding of his heart. The embrace was caring and gentle. But the arms themselves were strong. They belonged to the same man who had kissed her forehead last night—or whenever it was she had blown in here. But she must leave this house.

"What time is it?" she asked foolishly, wishing he would never change into the other Clayton

Madrone—just hold her like this forever, the two of them drifting into outer space, where there were no ups and no downs. . .just space and the privacy he obviously treasured.

" 'What time is it?' she asks me—it's coffee time—it's time I apologized for my brutish behavior. It's time I kissed you—isn't that how you planned to get your story?"

And then he thrust her from him roughly. "I'm sorry. I had no right." His voice could have come from Mars. "I have coffee ready. The guest bath is down the hall, two doors to the right. Your clothes will be dry when we've had a five o'clock snack."

Five o'clock! He had been fully dressed when she arrived and had not been to bed. He must keep hoot-owl time! But Kitty dared not make a comment, for the moment of intimacy was over between them. He was again the withdrawn stranger. She wondered who or what in life had hurt him so much. And what could he mean by "get your story"?

Kitty stole a look at the deceptive gauntness of his body, knowing how strong the arms were. The dark hair and beard reminded her of someone. Had she seen him somewhere, or was it his similarity to two men she admired? That was it—he was a cross between James Stewart and Abraham Lincoln. But young Abe had been dubbed "Honest Abe." If "honest" meant *open*, there was no similarity in the personalities.

"That's the first time I've seen you scowl," he grinned.

"And that's the first time I've seen you smile! You must be very happy in your misery—some kind of a happy hermit!"

For a moment, Clayton Madrone looked at her in something akin to surprise. He took one step toward her, then spun on his heel and headed for what must be the kitchen. Kitty wrapped the robe about herself quickly and ran down the hall in search of the guest bath.

The bathroom was a surprise. Kitty glanced around her in appreciation. The walls were cactus-green, blending with the deeper green of the tiled shower and floor. But what captured her attention was the definite woman's touch of cologne, talc, and bubble bath. There was an assortment of light-weight polyester dressing gowns hanging in a little recessed nook. So the hermit was married! That should relieve any anxieties she felt. Instead, Kitty felt an undeniable sense of disappointment—then anger. At him. And herself.

All the questions about Clayton Madrone's private life and his marital status melted away when Kitty caught sight of herself in the three-way mirror above the washbasin. Could that ghostly creature be herself? No wonder the man viewed her with suspicion—and undoubtedly scorn. Her waist-length, heavy brown hair was always a source of ag-gravation. Recently she had taken to pinning it loosely on top of her head—at first to get it out of her way and then because she liked the more sophis-ticated look it gave her innocent-looking face. Not that it stayed there long at a time. Unlike its owner, Kitty's hair had never affected passivity. It had a will of its own. Let a window open and it came tumbling down to coil about her shoulders, which was where it was now. In the absence of a blow-dry, every hair seemed to have taken off in a dif-ferent direction. Set in the pallor of her pale face, the gray, oval-shaped eyes—always too large for her face—looked even more quizzical than usual beneath the dark brows. And the bathrobe hung on her too-tall, too-thin figure like a scarecrow's garment. Her generous mouth, too often pursed in thought, was now drawn in a colorless line across her face. She had work to do!

After a quick shower Kitty felt better. A few strokes of the hairbrush did wonders, and her skin, still rosy from its scrub, glowed beneath the thin coating of moisturizer. A dust of powder. An upward sweep with the blusher. She liked the raspberry lip gloss so well that she applied a second coat. Kitty was about to turn away from the mirror when her eyes came to rest on the filmy robes. Didn't her new face deserve more than a man's bathrobe—which was beginning to scratch? Daringly, she reached for the first one. She slipped her arms into the wide sleeves and knotted the heavy silk cord about her waist. *The colors are just right*, she thought with a smile—raspberry to match her lip gloss blended with rose-pink to match her cheeks. Pleased with the effect, she closed the door behind her and hurried down the hall before she could lose her courage.

Reaching the living room before Clayton Madrone, Kitty whistled softly for John Doe. When the dog did not respond, she guessed that her host had let him go exploring while he prepared coffee. She supposed there was no harm in doing some exploring on her own. *Surely her host would have no objection to her admiring his taste in art*, she thought as she looked around the enormous, built-for-comfort room. He must be a man of means, for the furniture, the polished wood paneling, and the assortment of

copper, brass, and pewter vases were not the kind
one picked up at a swap meet. But it was his book
collection which took her eye. Her first surprise was
at finding an enormous Bible lying open on top of
the cluttered desk. Cushioned by what looked like
unopened mail, the Bible obviously had had recent
use. Kitty moved on to examine the other books,
wondering what taste so strange a man (correction,
couple) would have in reading. *Faith of Our Fathers,
Pilgrim's Progress in Religion, Religious Practices
Among the African Tribes.* What was this man,
anyway? She had called him a *hermit. Monk* would
be more like it. But before she could take her thinking further, her eyes caught sight of the author's
name, the same in each case: *Clayton. Clayton
Madrone wrote all of these?* His name was on them
as proof. And yet she was unable to put the books
and this man of many moods together.

She reached for one of the books, and the wide
sleeve of her robe caught a sheet of paper on the
desk, causing it to fall to the floor. Kitty retrieved
it. Then, as she was about to lay it on the desk, the
title caught her attention—and then the byline:
Religion Among the American Indians Today, by
Clayton Madrone.

A writer. This man was a writer! And apparently
a well-known one. That accounted for his thinking
she would recognize him . . .

"Did you find what you're looking for?"

Kitty had not heard the door open, and the stern
voice startled her. "I—I—you have to believe me, I
wasn't meddling—"

"Maybe they don't call it that in your line of
work."

"My line of work—" Kitty turned around slowly.

"I'm not an enemy. Or a spy. I don't even have a job. I'm not an anything!"

"Oh, yes, you are!" The words were spoken softly, but they vibrated with emotion. "You are a very beautiful woman—and I have misjudged you." He set the coffee tray down and made a step toward her. His face was still stern, but his eyes glowed with a mixture of interest and admiration. And, behind the glow, there was a loneliness.

Kitty felt an unfamiliar desire to reach out and touch him—to make him smile, to ease his loneliness. But this was dangerous thinking, she knew.

"Your wife—" The words sounded foolish. She swallowed and tried again. "She surely equipped the bath nicely—"

"I have no wife." The words, softly spoken, were bitter. And they served to turn him from her. "Come and have your coffee before it gets cold," he said matter-of-factly as he picked up the pot and poured two cups. He buttered toast, handed it to her, and said, "There's cactus jelly in the stone jar if you'd like to try it."

After that he was silent. Casting for something to say which would break the uncomfortable silence, Kitty complimented the house. Clayton made no sign of hearing. Then she asked where John Doe was.

Clayton Madrone set down his coffee cup and turned to face her. "I still haven't figured you out," he said slowly. "How long have you had that dog?"

"Three days. I picked him up at the pound—"

"*Her!*"

His laugh came again—low, mellow, and this time genuinely amused. "Then you didn't know the dog was going to whelp?"

"Whelp?" Kitty echoed.

"Give birth."

"But that can't happen—I—we—*puppies*?"

"The same. John Doe, if you insist the dog is male, is about to become a father!"

Kitty was breathing hard, but none of the air seemed to be reaching her lungs. How was she going to cope? She had yet to reach her destination and, once there, it was entirely possible she would have to make a U-turn back. Back where? Her future was so uncertain. Her resources were so small. It had seemed like a good idea to have a dog along for the long trip. The dog's gentle manner and Kitty's natural love for animals had prompted her decision at the animal shelter. One lick of the nameless dog's affectionate tongue had won her heart. But a litter of Baby Does was another matter entirely.

"What am I to do?" She looked desperately at the man who had provided shelter but not hospitality.

"Do? Well, if this were *my* problem—and it isn't!—I'd rename the dog. Then let nature take care of the rest. You won't have long to wait. That's why she's so lethargic."

"I've got to get out of here. Where *am* I? You never got around to answering that."

"So I didn't," he said lazily. "You, my dear, are a guest of the 'Circle Right Ranch'."

Kitty searched his face for signs that he was joking. Seeing none, she continued to stare. Something in his manner said that he was enjoying himself.

"Stop staring and drink your coffee before it gets cold!" The words were a command. Kitty drained the cup and looked up at the rugged face, wondering how to approach him for help in getting her car back onto the road.

His blue eyes met her wide gray ones. "Did anybody ever tell you that you have eyes like a curious
kitten who has just unrolled a ball of yarn and is
wondering how to rewind it?"

At the shake of her head, Clayton Madrone said,
as if deciding an important issue, "Most of the Indian women in these parts have names taken from
nature, so I've got it! 'Kitten Eyes,' that's you."

How could one dislike a man who amused and,
in some strange way, flattered her? But how could
one trust or even like a man who ran hot and cold
so unpredictably? He was the strangest man she'd
ever met . . . or were all men like him? She had met
so few. Maybe all of them were infuriatingly rude—
and maddeningly attractive. No, this one was different. His sudden changes were born of an aching
heart. And that may have been the most important
of the reasons she had for wanting to get out of here.
Now—before it was too late.

It was already too late! Kitty realized that she had
been so engrossed in her new surroundings—no, the
man who dominated them—that she did not realize
the world outside had turned pink with the promise
of a desert sunrise. Neither had she heard a car drive
into the graveled driveway and stop. The slamming
of a car door, the sound of hurrying feet, and then
the impatient knock on the front door brought her
back to reality.

Help had come! That was good. But her hopes
were short-lived. The door burst open before
Clayton had more than risen from his chair. And
there stood one of the most incredibly beautiful
women Kitty had ever seen.

Did she imagine it, or did his face whiten at the
sight of the dusky-skinned beauty? It was obvious

that the woman had eyes only for him. Her full lips were curved in laughter, reserved just for him— the kind that held an invitation with a promise, an invitation which was repeated in the quick, nervous curving of her brightly enameled nails as they combed through her stylishly short blue-black hair. A few quick steps and the curvy body—made more so by the tight fit of the designer jeans—was across the room. And Clayton Madrone was caught in a tight embrace.

"*Darling!*" But even as she embraced him, the woman's dark eyes swept the room around her, assessing the situation and weighing Kitty as a possible rival.

"How cozy," she murmured, her voice saying that Kitty posed no threat. She ran a playful hand through Clayton's hair. Then, raising her voice, she called, "Come on in, Rhett, and see what this benevolent man's taken in this time!"

Kitty felt herself color beneath the intended insult. She longed to escape, knowing that things would get worse, no matter how her host handled the situation.

"Kitty Fairfield, Colette Drubay," Clayton said, his tone telling her nothing. "Kitty—Miss Fairfield's car is ditched—"

"And you just happened to be passing by—how convenient!" There was mockery in the light laugh.

"I didn't just happen to be *anywhere*! I was at home when she came, which is fortunate. She was half-drowned!"

"And you toweled her off, and she purred for you! You surely should know, Miss Fairfield—pardon, it's *Kitty* that Clay calls you, isn't it? You should know that he takes in anything that scratches at his door.

Let's see, there was the sparrow that never learned
to fly...the baby coyote...and, *ugh!* the most
horrible-looking lizard. But they were so helpless,
you understand?"

"That's enough, Colette!" Clayton's voice was
dangerously low. This woman was everything Kitty
disliked in another woman. But she was his friend—
undoubtedly a very *close* friend!—and he had a right
to choose his associates. Kitty had caused him
enough trouble already. If only she could think of
some way to make a quick getaway—

But it was too late. The front door was blocked
by a man so large, it seemed to her, that his shadow
caused half the room to go into an eclipse. Another
introduction was in progress and she, Kitty...Miss
Fairfield..."Kitten Eyes"...or whoever she was,
had not found her tongue to acknowledge the previous one. What name did Clayton say? Rhett Dawson?

"Just call me Rhett, Kitty," the giant was saying.
"We're a pretty informal lot around here. Right,
gang?"

"Right." Clayton and Colette repeated. But nothing
in their voices or their previous manners agreed
with what Rhett Dawson had said.

Kitty murmured something. She was never sure
what. She was too busy looking at the remote handsomeness of Clayton Madrone, so like the saguaro
cacti around them—hard to reach because of the armor of thorns, protection against the tender inva-
sion that might bring out the rare blossom; the ripe
beauty of Colette Drubay, who was obviously in
love with him; and now this third member of the
new trio, whose face she had had little chance to
examine.

Turning slightly toward Rhett Dawson, Kitty's eyes met his. Deep-blue, they looked out of place in the sun-darkened face. The suntan, she noted, ended in an area of white just below the hairline, visible only since he had pushed back the large, expensive-looking felt hat. His boots were high-heeled, adding needlessly to his height, and they shone with a blinding new gloss. Plaid shirt. Good jeans, revealing slightly parentheses-shaped legs that said he had spent a lot of time astride a horse. The All-American Cowboy. And yet something bothered her. Maybe it was the nervous fumbling with the wide brim of his hat. Was he the typical "Rhinestone Cowboy" who saw ranching as a hobby? Or maybe he wasn't a rancher at all—

"I'm relieved to find you're all right, Kitty. I checked on you, knowing it was about time for you to be getting here. Expected you'd come by 'Promenade Ranch'. . ."

He knew I would be getting here. But how? Her eyes must have widened the way Clayton Madrone described them, for the newcomer was answering her unasked question. "I'm your neighbor to the north," he explained, his eyes friendly, his countenance open—giving Kitty the sudden feeling that here was a young man who wore his heart on his sleeve.

"I'm the neighbor to the south, the way he's explaining the layout of the land," Clayton's voice broke in.

Kitty nodded numbly. Here where houses were miles apart, she was meeting too many people too fast. Something seemed irregular, but she was unable to put her finger on it—or give it any more thought. There was silence. Was she supposed to say something? "So I'm in the middle," she observed.

And, glancing at the faces around her, Kitty had the feeling that she was right. In more ways than one.

Clayton went to the kitchen for fresh coffee. As the door closed behind him, Kitty asked to be excused. "I must change—"

"Oh, you really shouldn't." Colette's voice carried a cutting edge beneath its sweetness. "The color does more for you than it does for me. But Clay likes it—so—" She shrugged delicately.

"My things were wet," Kitty said stiffly. "Thank you for its use." Then, turning from Colette, she said, "And I thank you, Mr.—Rhett—I appreciate your checking on my safety. But," she frowned, "you have not explained how you knew I was expected. Nobody knew except the attorney."

"It was Mr. Gotschalk who asked me to keep an eye out for you. The house is not really—well, you'll see it for yourself. And it was your wagon in the ditch?"

"I'm afraid so," Kitty said. "It was in a river when John—Jane Doe and I fled. I was in such a rush—" At that Kitty's hands flew to her face to muffle a scream she felt rising from the area of her heart and lodging in her throat, choking off the air.

Rhett Dawson was at her side immediately. "What's wrong, Kitty? Let me help you!"

Hardly aware of the protective arm around her shoulders, Kitty leaned weakly against him to keep from crumpling to the floor. "My purse," she whispered. "I left it in the car—"

Rhett's forehead knotted in concentration. "There was nothing there that looked like a purse," he said slowly. "I did wonder how these came to be in the seat, but that's all there was."

He handed Kitty her traveler's checks—the only cash she had in the world. That was a great relief. Even so, they had not been the most valuable item in the handbag.

"Where could it have gone? I—I—"

"What was in it? We'll find it, I'm sure." Rhett's voice was reassuring, but it did not take away the terrible fear that gripped her heart.

"All my identification—everything I need to claim my father's property is there. I don't know what I can do—you'll have to excuse me."

And with that, she fled to the guest bath. Her own blouse and skirt were hanging in the nook from which she had taken the robe. The "other Clayton"

had hung them there, the one Kitty felt she alone
had come to know in such a short while. But she
was an intruder here, unwanted and interfering
with the writing he seemed to take so seriously.
Anyway, she was able to establish little more than
slight contact with the magnificent man when the
angry one stepped in to take his place. She wondered
which side of him appealed to Colette Drubay and
just what she was to him. Something unwholesome,
no doubt.

At the door of the living room she paused, making an effort to smooth out the wrinkles in her skirt.
The little wrinkles were permanent—supposedly
practical and certainly worn a lot this year. But a
natural fastidiousness within her rebelled at the
larger ones that tattled of the long, hard ride even
after their soaking.

It was hopeless. Straightening, Kitty was about to
join the others when Clayton's voice, pitched pur-
posely low, reached her ears. "I thought the film
was finished, Colette. And that our arrangement was
finished, too."

"Oh, it is—I mean, they are. But I needed to pick
up some of my things." Colette's voice was velvety
soft and carried with it the sound of motion. Kitty
could almost see her moving toward Clayton. When
the girl spoke, Kitty was certain she was right.
"And—there, don't pull away, Darling! You know
you're attracted to me."

"Don't, Colette! I've been hurt too much already.
We've had this conversation before—and you still
seem to cling to that romantic notion that physical
attraction and love are one and the same."

Kitty could almost see the lacquered nails comb-
ing Clayton's hair instead of her own. Her slender

arms would be around his neck, molding her to him. Embarrassed, Kitty wondered what she should do. Certainly this was no time to break in on the conversation. She was wondering about a back exit when there was a muffled scream of rage.

"How dare you! How *dare* you cast me aside like an old shoe!" Colette's voice was no longer intimate and appealing.

"Those were my lines, remember?" Clayton's voice sounded tired.

"It's that little stray you took in, isn't it?" she hissed. "Pretending to lose her way—and you fell for it! It's the oldest game in the world and you fell for it!"

Clayton's voice was dangerously low. "I was trained by an expert."

The front door slammed and Kitty heard the click of high heels on the concrete porch, followed by the banging shut of a car door. A spurt of gravel said Colette was gone.

Kitty waited a few seconds before entering the room. Clayton stood looking out the window, his back to her. Again she admired the broad-shouldered, firmly muscled body—well over six feet, she judged. In his late twenties? Probably, because his face, though mature, still showed the freshness of manhood. There was raw strength about him. Hard-boned. As well as hard-nosed!

The thought made her smile, and Clayton turned just in time to see the smile. Surprisingly, he smiled back and then moved toward her slowly in the easy, swivel-hipped walk that placed him in the saddle instead of at a typewriter.

"I don't know how much you heard—"

When he paused, "She's very beautiful," Kitty said.

"She's an actress," he replied, as if that explained both her beauty and behavior. "Pour yourself some more coffee and your car should be here by then. Rhett's gone for it. He came in this morning with Colette but caught a ride back with the Colonel."

"The Colonel?"

Clayton picked up his coffee, muttered that it was cold, and set it down. "Colonel Witham—you mean, you don't know? That he goes with the property?"

Kitty shook her head. "I know you don't believe me, but I've never been here. I'm who I say—and I don't know anything about the country, its people—anything—"

When he said nothing, Kitty continued, "My father left the ranch to me and I'm here to see it. Nothing more. And I see now that I shouldn't have come. I lost my way. I lost my shoes, my purse, my dog—" Kitty stopped short, seized by the crazy idea of adding, "and my heart!"

"The shoes are no problem. My sister left a pair of moccasins about your size that will do until you can get to the trading post. The purse—" Clayton frowned and appeared to be deciding what to say, "well, it's strange that it disappeared. Stranger still that the person who took it would leave your traveler's checks—if they were in the bag."

When Kitty nodded that they were, Clayton admitted that it was doubly strange. "But," he said, brightening, "the dog's fine—stretched out on a rug in the kitchen, resting as expectant mothers are supposed to. Do you know anything about delivering puppies?"

Kitty felt a slow blush creeping up from her neck to stain her cheeks. She had never discussed such matters with a man. And he was expecting an answer. "Why, I thought that was her job," she said finally.

The words sounded so artless that Kitty expected him to laugh or be cross. Instead, he said quietly, "Sometimes there's a need to help, and we're too far away out here to call a vet."

"I'm in a mess. Wouldn't you say, Clayton?" Kitty asked in a wee-small voice.

"I'll help you." His words were gruff but gentle.

"Oh, would you? I mean, if I stay?" His words had filled the vast sky with a luminous sun that she was sure wasn't there before. She could feel its warmth in her veins, giving her new life. When she turned to face Clayton, she was sure that he felt the same way. It was as if they had transfused each another with a newborn happiness.

"I shouldn't have been so rough on you." Clayton's voice was apologetic and more—much more. There was an intimacy that made Kitty long to spring into his arms. She had felt so comfortable there before—so safe. What a frightening thought! Women were not supposed to feel such things.

To cover her confusion, Kitty murmured, "I understand. You need solitude to do your writing, and I guess so famous a person has a lot of reporters and fans—is that why you grew the beard?"

Clayton's laugh was so genuine that it was contagious. It demanded company. And, ridiculously, Kitty found herself laughing with him, having no idea at all what they were laughing about. "I'm not *that* famous, Kitten Eyes," he said. "And yet you've come close to the truth. You amaze me—so unaffected and unpretentious, but filled with insight. As a matter of fact, yes, I did grow the beard at a time when..."

When his voice trailed off and stopped, Kitty knew that he had reached the part of his life which was painful. It had something to do with people—no one person in particular—who had managed to get too close to him and tampered with his work and his heart.

"I'm sorry," she began then stopped. After all, if Clayton wanted her to know more, he would tell her. Questions would be out of order and would only make him suspicious of her again, or push him back into the protective armor of silence. "I'm sorry for all the inconvenience I've caused. And I hope I've convinced you that I'm not here for your story, I'm no writer, but I *am* a reader. I read so much when Mother was ill that books became my only friends. Would you believe you're the first person I've talked to except to exchange a 'Good morning' when I paid my rent or spoke to my mother's doctor?"

"I would believe it, yes. You see, I don't talk with people either, although our reasons are different." He reached across the table and took her hand, stroking it gently at first, finger by finger, and then tightening his grip. "Kitten—"

Whatever he had been about to say was interrupted by the sound of a motor. Clayton dropped her hand almost roughly and stood up. "Could be the linesmen coming to check on the phones—no, it's Dawson with your car. Let me get the shoes from the closet, and I'll send some books along for you to read."

But he made no move to go. Glancing out the window at the sound of tires on gravel, he said quickly, "How much do you know about the property, your father, and the attorney?"

"Nothing. Nothing about Rhett either, of course—or this Colonel Witham. Is there something I should know?"

Instead of answering her directly, Clayton opened the closet door, drew out a pair of beaded moccasins, and then reached for several of his books. "I'll check in on you." His voice, muffled behind the pile of books, told her nothing. And his face, when she met his eyes, revealed nothing either.

A few minutes later Kitty was seated beside Rhett Dawson, with Jane Doe stretched out in the backseat of the car. Rhett had spread old sheets of plastic over the wet upholstery in the front. "And it was smart of you," he teased, "to keep the back end above water."

"Nothing I've done yet has been smart," Kitty replied. "I'm afraid I was a terrible nuisance to Clayton, and now I'm a bother to you."

"Only partially correct, Kitty. You might as well know now that anybody is a potential enemy to Clay. But, take *me* now—anybody's a potential friend!"

"You make me feel better." She was going to need a friend even if her stay was brief. It was good that she had Rhett as a neighbor. He seemed so open, uncomplicated, and willing to help her—almost too good to be true. Kitty stole a quick look at his profile. The straight nose pointed straight ahead. Like a bird of prey, he concentrated on the narrow road without moving a muscle. It was hard to imagine his doing anything impetuous—

reaching out suddenly to touch her the way Clayton did, for instance. But why in the world should she be comparing the two men? She forced herself to concentrate on the scenery beyond the car window.

"Oh, look! I didn't realize last night they were in bloom." Excitedly Kitty pointed to the creamy-white blossoms which seemed to have sprung from every perpendicular branch of the saguaros.

Rhett pushed his hat back, again showing the white line at the edge of his hair which must have avoided the sun. "The show's brief. The blooms die of thirst like everything else in the desert."

"But the plants don't. I remember reading that some of them live to be 200. And they bear fruit, don't they?"

Rhett did not meet her glance. "I'm surprised your host didn't share some of his sweetmeats made from the cactus fruit."

"He did—jelly. And it was delicious."

"He and his Indian friends exchange recipes and yarns and smoke the peacepipe together in general. Of course, he has his reasons. He's writing a book about their paganism, you know—oh, here we are. This is how you missed the road."

Paganism? Somehow this was not what Kitty gathered that Clayton had in mind, according to the title of his book. But it was of no concern to her. She was more curious about the three almost-hidden lanes which came together with only mailboxes to mark the intersection and then fanned out to the three adjoining ranches.

"The spreads are sort of pie-shaped," Rhett explained.

"Then we have to drive all this distance and double back to get in touch?"

Rhett wheeled the wagon onto the road between the other two—her road. Something in the ring of it gave her a sense of pride. And, in spite of the long, emotion-filled drama of yesterday, Kitty felt the same pull she had sensed before. Home. This was *home!*

Feeling Rhett's eyes on her, Kitty turned, causing him to redden. Watching him from the corner of her eye, she noticed that he kept fingering his hat nervously. Was he always so shy around women?

"There it is—the back road we take when there's an emergency." Rhett pointed to a narrow, dusty road that looked more like a trail linking the three ranches. "So if you need help—"

Kitty smiled. "I'm in the middle," she remembered.

"Better come to me. You'll be more welcome."

The two men did not like each other—that was obvious. She wondered why. In fact, it surprised her that Rhett would dislike anybody. He was so helpful, so ready to be a friend.

"We'll be coming up on the house soon, Kitty. And there's a lot you'll need to know. Just be cautious— not jumping into anything too soon, or taking anybody or anything for granted."

Something in his voice gave her a sense of foreboding, a feeling she tried to shake off in order to concentrate on his words. "Tell me more," she prompted when he was silent.

"Oh, nothing you should worry about—or maybe you should. Some strange things have been taking place around the ranch since your father died.

I've tried to keep an eye on it as much as time allowed, since Mr. Gotschalk left most of it up to me—"

"What do you mean, Rhett—left it up to you?"

Rhett negotiated a turn around a giant saguaro before answering. "I've taken too much for granted— like driving this morning without permission. But I wanted to make sure everything was in working condition." Kitty nodded her appreciation but said nothing, hoping not to interrupt his train of thought. "And I guess I thought you knew I was a junior partner with Gotschalk & Gotschalk—working only part-time and taking care of my stock the rest of the time."

The news surprised her somehow. Rhett wasn't the typical cowboy. But he was not the typical lawyer either. Asked to explain her thinking, Kitty would have been at a loss. It was just a feeling she had. She was about to inquire about the "strange happenings" when Rhett pointed again. "That's where your carpetbagger resides—there in the old cook shack. Or didn't you know about the Colonel?"

"Only that he goes with the property. I think that was how Clayton phrased it."

"He wouldn't if it were mine, though he's a harmless enough old coot, I used to think. An Englishman with no sense of humor."

Used to think. Kitty was about to ask Rhett what happened to change his mind but saw that he was looking ahead of them in surprise. She followed his gaze to where the cactus forest began to open up, giving way to the blueness of distant mountains. In the midst of the opening stood a house. Hers! It had to be. Kitty was both surprised and delighted with its native-stone quaintness. Symmetrical and square, centered by a heavy door, with boarded windows set in precise order on either side, this building reminded her of the beloved doll house she had had as a child.

But it was the sleek-looking automobile in front that seemed to have captured Rhett's attention. "That's odd," he said. "I didn't expect Mr. Gotschalk. Good thing he's here, though. You will need a key—"

When he hesitated, Kitty felt a sense of embarrassment. What must these people think of her? It was so obvious that she was unaccustomed to taking matters into her hands, planning ahead, or even knowing how. How had she expected to get into the house without a key? She was going to have to learn to think things through by herself eventually. Until then, it was good that she had Rhett to turn to.

The front door opened and the attorney came out to meet them. There was time for a quick appraisal before the introductions. He had an all-gray appearance. Gray pin-striped suit and matching tie. A few long strands of gray hair across the top of his head. Ashen skin. And somehow his behavior went with the all-over impression of grayness. Grave, cool, and formal. He extended a wafer-thin hand as Rhett said, "Mr. Gotschalk, this is our Kitty Fairfield."

Kitty took the cold hand. "The new owner of the 'Circle Left.' Let's go inside. This sun's for the young and foolish." The lawyer mopped his forehead after the handshake.

Mr. Gotschalk turned to walk up the graveled entrance, which was almost hidden by low-growing, dead vegetation. Kitty followed, aware that Rhett was close at her heels, as if about to push in front. Clearing his throat, he spoke over her head, "Partner!" Rhett's voice was low, and the title with which he addressed the attorney was informal, but the tone seemed to carry a note of urgency missed by her ear, as the older man stopped in his tracks.

Rhett pushed his hat back, then took it off and fanned himself. The motion was slow and lazy. But his words, Kitty thought, sounded hurried. "Mr. Gotschalk, as executor of the estate, you will want to establish identity, and while there is no doubt that Kitty Fairfield is the rightful owner—"

"He's going to be a successful lawyer. Very suspicious."

The attorney's words caused Rhett to color. "Please don't undo the impression I've tried to make, offering to be Kitty's Man Friday," he said lightly. "However, it seems that she's misplaced her identification. I will be responsible personally to see to it that we get copies made in due time—"

"It would be hard for me to think of you as an impostor, my dear," Mr. Gotschalk said kindly, "but," he sighed, "business is business. I'll need a copy of your birth certificate and a copy of your mother's death certificate. As I told you on the telephone, I have your father's death certificate. And, of course, there should be proof of your citizenship. I should have made all this clear."

"Oh, you did," Kitty said quickly. "And I had everything—and then—oh, I don't know what happened, but somebody must have taken my purse."

Near tears, she tried to explain. Mr. Gotschalk's expression did not change. It was hard to tell what he was thinking. And it was hard to imagine what would happen to her and Jane Doe if some technicality prevented them from lodging here.

"There'll be no problem—just a little delay," Rhett reassured her when Mr. Gotschalk was silent. "Meantime, you can stay with me—"

"Oh, no! I couldn't possibly. What I mean is, I—well, I can't consider that."

Rhett's brown fingers rolled up the brim of his hat as he twisted it around nervously. His face had reddened again. "Please don't misunderstand, Kitty. I only meant the use of one of my spare rooms. You haven't been a cowgirl long enough to understand our Western hospitality. My intentions are strictly honorable."

It was Kitty's turn to be embarrassed. She murmured an appreciation, then added, "If I can only stay here until things are settled—"

"*Alone?*" Kitty was never sure which of the men said the word with such emphasis. At the time, it sounded like both.

"I have some supplies. I have the dog. And," she said, brightening, "there's the Colonel."

Rhett's laugh did not sound amused. "One about as helpful as the other. But I'll be responsible for her if it's okay by you, Gotschalk—both ways. I'll vouch she's who she says and I'll look after her needs if the lady will allow. Kit?"

Kitty smiled. "You've been more than kind. I don't know how to thank you other than—"

Before she could finish an invitation to a future meal, the attorney was turning the key in the lock. The matter seemed to be settled, although Kitty wondered what tipped the scales in her favor. *Maybe that's the way with lawyers,* she thought, realizing that she knew as little about them as she knew about men in general.

Giving them what she felt was a rather benign smile, Kitty followed the two men into a long hall, dark now because the three doors leading off it were closed. Curious, she opened the one to the right and found herself looking at her own reflection in a full-length mirror with natural lighting from above. A slatted blind over the skylight let her see clearly a slender young woman whose enormous eyes were wide with questions. But they did not show her doubt and uncertainty or the fear that she would be unable to cope alone.

The second door led to a bedroom and the third into a large, old-fashioned living room. It was here, she decided, that her father must have spent most of his time. The other two rooms were untouched since the house was built, Kitty guessed. But the living room, though in need of a little paint and a lot of cleaning, said that this was the lived-in part. Books, magazines, and newspapers were stacked according to date, though layered with dust. The large window overlooking what once had been a cactus garden in back made the room look light and airy. Of course, there was a need for drapes.

Kitty, caught up in planning, was unaware that the men had moved on into the kitchen. It was Jane Doe's wet nose on her palm and a little whine from the animal that reminded her that the two of them were alone. "Did you think I'd forgotten you, pal?" Kitty said, patting the sleek, fawn-colored head. The dog looked so genuinely pleased that Kitty leaned down and hugged her neck. "We'll need each other, you and I. Now, let's explore the kitchen."

Jane Doe whined again, almost as if she were in pain. Remembering the dog's condition, Kitty was glad Clayton had said he would help. That might depend on the mood he was in. But there was Rhett. She needed somebody desperately, for, although she loved this place, Kitty sensed more than just challenge...something truly foreboding....

4

Kitty, always an early riser, awoke the next morning to find the sun shining through the freshly washed window. She bounded out of bed and switched on the small table radio she located beneath a mountain of notebooks (all of them filled up with what must have been her father's handwriting).

Expecting to hear music or news, she was surprised when a rather pleasant, faintly familiar voice said, "And we can be reassured of God's eternal presence by the number of passages included in the Bible which comfort in time of fear.

Our Creator does nothing by accident, and the 365 references reinforce that claim. That's one for each day of the year! In closing, may I share with you Proverbs 9:10: 'The fear of the Lord is the beginning of wisdom.' The Lord make His face to shine upon you this day!"

Mr. Gotschalk had said in parting last night that he would be here at 9:30 with papers for her to go over. The radio announcer, with a background of a softly sung hymn, gave the time as 9:00 A.M., which meant, Kitty supposed, that the Lord had been causing His face to shine for several hours now—while she slept. Kitty knew very little about what she had heard referred to as "His mysterious ways," but if God could dispel fear such as she had experienced last night after Mr. Gotschalk and Rhett left . . . well, it was worth thinking about. It was fear that made her, tired as she was, dig in and start scrubbing away a layer of accumulated dirt from the windows. She could have just imagined the tapping at the door. But if it was just her imagination working overtime, why had Jane Doe barked? The dog's angry growls continued after the tapping stopped . . . so it was real.

Kitty shuddered, remembering. Without irreverence, she wished she knew how to contact the man who read the Bible verse. He deserved a "Thank you" to have made her feel less guilty about her fear, saying it was the start of wisdom.

Realizing that she had been standing idly instead of getting dressed, Kitty hurried toward the midget-size shower. But, even as she felt the delicious prickle of the cold water, her mind kept pulling her back to the voice she had heard. Then, as she was toweling dry, another thought took over. Kitty realized that she had uncovered the first clue as to what her father was like. Any man who preferred listening to a morning devotional over a sportscast giving the standing of the sparring teams in the major league tryouts was, to say the least, different—as different as the man who read the Bible aloud so early in the morning. For some reason, she liked the idea. But it would go better with coffee. She hurried to the kitchen.

A few minutes later she was pouring a cup for herself and one for Mr. Gotschalk, who had climbed from his car and checked his watch before knocking. Kitty had the distinct feeling that had he been five seconds early, he would have waited.

Kitty was as ready to defend her newly acquired ability to cope with the desert as a mother defends its young. Mr. Gotschalk, however, solemnly stirred his coffee, said he trusted she had slept well, and then said sternly, "Now, let's get on with business." With that, he produced a large brown envelope and began spreading legal documents and photographs on the table.

"Yes, let's," she murmured, not looking at the papers. Instead, she picked up a photograph. "Is this my father?"

Of course she knew the answer before the attorney said it was, "presumably"—although he had never met his client. Something seemed wrong with that. But Kitty was too engrossed with the dark handsomeness of the man in the picture to think the lawyer-client relationship through.

"I'd have recognized him." Kitty was unaware

that she had spoken aloud until there was the sound of in-taken breath. She realized then that Mr. Gotschalk's eyes were studying her.

"I understood that you did not know your father."

"Oh, I didn't, not personally. I only knew—" Kitty paused, wondering herself what she had been about to say. Of course she hadn't known her father. The feeling of familiarity had to be due to the heavy eyebrows that arched quizzically against the high forehead, just as hers did. But her eyes were like Mother's.

"There is a resemblance, isn't there?" Kitty said.

"More pronounced in this photograph," Mr. Gotschalk answered, handing her a picture of a very youthful couple standing beneath a giant saguaro. Laughing and squinting against the sun, they looked carefree, happy, and in love. Kitty recognized her mother immediately and, having seen the previous photograph, knew that the handsome man was her father. With one arm he drew his wife possessively to him, almost throwing her off-balance with the embrace. With the other he proudly cradled a bit of blanket-wrapped humanity that had to be herself.

"I see no pronounced resemblance to *myself* here," Kitty laughed, the picture making her feel lighthearted. It was good to know that Mother and Daddy had been happy, if only briefly. They looked so rock-sure of their love. What happened?

When Mr. Gotschalk did not speak, Kitty looked at him. "This *is* me my father's holding?" she said, wondering why she felt a need to convince him.

"That we will need to verify by some dates, I suppose—" .

"Verify? I can understand your need for identification before surrendering the deed. But there can be no question about another possible heir. I was their only child—"

Without a coloring of doubt, Kitty had begun. But, even as she spoke, a strange possibility came to her, causing her to stop. When at length she spoke, her voice was small and strained.

"Is there a chance that there were other children—I mean from my father's second marriage?"

He was silent for a terrifying moment, his face very grave and serious. Then, to her amazement, the man stretched a pale hand across the table and touched her hand. "We must ascertain that there were no other children from the union of the two you call your parents—"

"They *are* my parents!" Kitty said, snatching her hand away. How dare this man cast any doubt on her birth! "I have their marriage certificate—I'm sorry, I *had* it—"

Mr. Gotschalk drained his cup and rose from the small table. "Try not to worry, Miss Fairfield. You have my solemn assurance that you will get your share. There are matters, however, which we must investigate. Some information which I should have had previously has now surfaced."

"You mean—this place may not be mine?"

Mr. Gotschalk looked uncomfortable. "Now, now, let's not jump to conclusions. But the fact is that—well, Mr. Fairfield and I had no personal contact except by telephone and an envelope he mailed once I had agreed to be his executor. At that time I did not know of his other wife—and child."

"You mean I have a half-brother or sister?" Kitty

waited with bated breath, her heart hammering against her rib cage. The thought had never occurred to her, and it was too new for her to determine her feelings.

"I really should not have brought the matter up at this time." Mr. Gotschalk hesitated and then continued, "But to answer your question, yes. What you possibly have somewhere is a half-brother by a previous marriage."

Kitty gasped. "You mean he—my father—was married *three* times instead of two?"

"No, he was never remarried after the separation from your mother. You knew, I presumed, that they were never divorced. There was only a legal separation, which in fact entitles you to the property without question—unless the child by his former marriage somehow manages—but that is unlikely to happen. The previous wife and son were out of touch—"

Kitty's whole world went out of focus. Through the kitchen window from which she had stripped the soiled curtains during last night's insomnia she saw a small cluster of horses standing statue-still around a Joshua tree, as if posed for a painting. Then they melted away in a wash of watercolor. The blue of the sky diluted before her very eyes and, in her shock, the down-slung loops of wire on the power poles loped like camels across the burning desert. It was all untrue. Everything her mother had said was untrue. And in that strange moment Kitty felt closer to her father than her mother.

5

Kitty lay wide-eyed and staring at the ceiling. What was the meaning of Mr. Gotschalk's news? Why had her mother kept the half-brother, if there was one, a secret? And why had she given the impression that Kitty's father had remarried after, as her mother explained it, deserting his wife and child?

Life is strange, she mused in the darkness. At first she had been unable to believe the unexpected legacy. Then she was unable to believe herself capable of breaking through the shell of passivity in which her mother had encased her. And now she was unable to accept the possibility that she might lose the house and acreage she had come to love already. At first sight of it there had been a sense of great elation. For the first time in her life there was born inside her a keen and nervous excitement. An itch to scrub, clean, paint—make a home. Here was a chance to prove herself—and please somebody. Even in her disappointment, she refused to admit why it was important that Clayton Madrone change his mind about her. It didn't matter anyway. Mr. Gotschalk knew more, she felt, than he told her. Her time here was limited.

Kitty's thinking was interrupted by an uneasy whine from Jane Doe, who lay on a blanket beside the bed. Oh, no! There it was, the same *tap-tap-tapping* of the previous night. A large mesquite bush, which needed removing, could be blowing against the door. Only there was no wind, just a soft blossom-scented breeze coming in through the open window. Maybe she should close the window.

A bang, as if some heavy object had been thrown against the back door, made up her mind. As noiselessly as possible, Kitty slipped from between the sheets she had laundered today—noting, even in her fear, their sun-dried freshness—and eased the window down. Somewhere a hungry-sounding coyote wailed, sending a chill down her spine even though the room had grown stuffy.

Finally all was quiet except for the contented snores of the dog, who had become her shadow already. Getting Jane Doe had been the only smart thing she had done so far. Or was that smart either? How in the world would she manage if there was trouble with delivering the puppies—providing

Clayton was in one of his dark moods? Thinking of Clayton made her wonder if the telephones were in working order. It was too late to try it tonight. He would be writing. And what was there to say anyway? A call would be an aggressive move.

The thought set her thinking of her mother again. Mother had been the "second wife." It was she who cautioned Kitty against being forward, showing her feelings, or responding too quickly even when a man—whose role it was to be the aggressor—made an overture of kindness. "Be on guard," she had said over and over, as if any communication with persons of the opposite sex placed her in enemy territory.

One scene came back in particular—a scene between Mother and Grandmother, neither of whom was aware that the thin waif she was at six had slipped between the banisters on the way to the kitchen for a glass of milk.

"You have no choice but to let her have the gift, I suppose." Grandmother's voice was low and so sad that it made Kitty want to cry. "The child will never know that it's a replica of the house itself. We are fortunate, my dear, that she was too young to remember, and not suffer the way you did when your father left. There will always be women like that—"

Mother's sobs had stopped Grandmother—and broken Kitty's heart. "Don't cry, Mommy, don't cry!" she had wanted to say, winding her arms around her mother's still-lovely neck. Instead, she watched her grandmother reach out to comfort her. But it did not stop her mother's sobbing. They simply clung together, two bitter, heartbroken women . . .

The memory, which had lingered frighteningly, caused an unidentifiable fear to rise up within her now. But for the first time, Kitty wondered if a part of their unhappiness could have been of their own making. Could the voice on the radio have been right? Caution, which eventually became fear, had been so instilled that it dominated her life. But now, if she could rid herself of the destructive fears and hang onto the "wise" ones, would she be able to live a more productive life than Mother and Grandmother Cramer? Daddy must have put some value on that kind of thinking. He listened. And so would she. Tomorrow.

Eventually she slept.

Jane Doe's wet nose on her cheek awakened Kitty. "So early? Let's sleep a little while yet." But her soothing tone did not encourage the dog back onto her blanket. Instead, there was an insistent whine that Kitty recognized.

Once the dog was at the back door, Kitty saw a faint glow in the east. For some reason her sense of adventure and determination had returned. Quickly she pulled on a pair of old jeans and a cotton blouse. After a cup of coffee, she would tackle the kitchen first, she decided. Even while the kettle gave out a merry whistle of readiness, Kitty searched for rags and whatever else her father may have had for cleaning purposes. When one layer of grime was off, she paused only long enough to measure instant coffee and pour water into the cup. Breakfast here, she decided, would have to be a movable feast—no more sitting down. She would grab whatever she could whenever she could and keep up the scrubbing rhythm she was so enjoying!

Jane Doe scratched to be let in. Kitty took a quick

break to feed her, then opened a can of orange juice and drank it standing up. Then she went back to her work. The walls were finished. The sink shone. Now, the oven.

It, she found, was in worse shape than anything she had worked on. At that, it looked better than *she* did, Kitty thought with a smile of amusement. Her hair had tumbled down. Her hands were blackened. And from the corner of her eye she could spot soot on the tip of her nose. But she felt wonderful! This was more than the dollhouse Daddy had sent, because she knew now what the conversation she had overheard meant. Oh, yes, it was a far greater gift. This was the real thing, not the replica. And nobody was going to take it from her, Kitty resolved. *Nobody!*

With that firm resolve, she worked all the more industriously. In no time the oven looked ready for a chocolate cake and the kitchen linoleum glistened like a newly minted coin. "Okay, bedroom, here we come!"

Kitty stopped long enough to tie a kerchief around her hair and toss Jane Doe a dog biscuit. Then the two of them went into the cluttered bedroom. Deciding to tackle the bedside table first, she began to heap the pile of notebooks and ancient seed catalogs on the floor. Undoubtedly all of it would be discarded, but she would go through it beforehand. She was tempted to take a break and leaf through what must be her father's notes. But a break might interrupt her flow of energy, and the sun was climbing higher.

Tired but elated, Kitty glanced at her watch. It was 8:55! The devotional!

Almost tripping over the pile of papers in her

haste, Kitty reached the radio in a single leap and turned the knob. "Oh, I hope I haven't missed him!"

Fortunately, she hadn't. But, unfortunately, she heard only the close' of the program, as she had yesterday. It was the same pleasing voice and, as she had hoped, speaking again on the subject of fear. Soothing. Unraveling the sleeves of care. As if the words were written and read especially for her.

" '*The fear of the Lord is clean, enduring forever*'— Psalm 19:9. Now may the Lord God be your strength today!"

Clean. Kitty tasted the word. Clean like her house. Although she was not exactly sure what the verse meant, it spoke to her of sparkling windows letting Somebody's face shine through. It spoke of forever-ness. And the reader had added muscle to the reading. Still puzzling over the familiarity of the voice, she vigorously scrubbed the table with warm, sudsy water, then waxed and polished the top. What improvement!

By noon the house was in much better order. Kitty walked from room to room enjoying the results of her long hours of work. Her back ached and she looked like a chimney sweep, but the reward was worth it.

In the kitchen she dusted her hands and sat down. No shower and no lunch until she had caught her breath. With a sense of pride she looked at the stretch of land framed by the large window. One day soon this would be hers—no strings attached. It was the first thing, actually, that Kitty had ever owned. Endless details lay between her and ownership, and undoubtedly the responsibilities would be heavy. But she had had the strength for this day, and that gave her an inner peace—a will to face whatever lay ahead. And there was a lot!

It occurred to Kitty that she had no idea how many of the horses she had seen belonged to her, if any. This could be open range country. Without fencing, the horses might have wandered in from either of the two adjoining ranches. She did recall that the "Circle Left" had 500 acres of land. That would require a lot of fencing...taxes would be high ...and come to think of it, wasn't there a mortgage? That would have to be checked into. Now that she was thinking more clearly, Kitty realized that dozens of matters needed checking out. Reaching for a pencil, she began a list of reminders. As it lengthened, she wondered about expenditures.

There was little hope that the purse would turn up, but Kitty was grateful that her traveler's checks were dropped by accident. If it was an accident, the thief was either a dunderhead or very considerate of his victims! She made a note to remind Mr. Gotschalk to help her obtain duplicates of her I.D. cards, then another regarding her driver's license. One ticket for driving without a permit was one too many on her slim budget; sleeping it out in jail would be more practical. Smiling at the thought, Kitty realized that she was getting to know herself better. Here she was in the biggest jam of her life, and she could smile about it! Somewhere underneath the colorless character she thought of herself as being, there was a sense of humor. It was like greeting a stranger.

"Hello, Kitten Eyes!" she said to herself. And then the smile did a fadeout, leaving her with the usual quizzical expression. Why, she wondered, had she used the name Clayton had given her instead of "Kit," the way Rhett shortened her name? Aware then of a gnawing in her stomach, Kitty began searching through her few supplies for the makings of a snack, letting the question go unanswered for now.

She had brought little food along, and most of it was gone except for some crackers and a can of sardines. Well, that was better than nothing. That was another thing she needed to know—surely there would have to be a grocery store somewhere closer than Tucson. Maybe there was a general store that stocked paint. New curtains would be nice, but they were probably more expensive than she could afford. Hardly a luxury, though, considering that the intruder could look right into her room. Her way of thinking caused Kitty to lay down the key she was about to use for opening the sardine can. The very thought that she had used a definite pronoun proved that she had accepted as a fact the presence of another human being stalking the premises at night. *The* intruder, not *an* intruder. Maybe her list was all wrong. Deciding which of the three men she should confide in ought to top the list.

Thoughtfully picking up the key again, Kitty slipped it over the tip flap of the lid. At the first twist there was a sharp rap on the front door, causing Jane Dce to try to lift her swollen body too quickly and lose her balance on the waxed floor. She skidded against Kitty in her unaccustomed awkwardness, a motion which knocked the partially open can from her hand, cutting through the flesh of her palm as it slid to the floor. There was an immediate spurt of blood and the sickening scent of fish oil.

When the rap was repeated, Kitty hurried to the door. It did not occur to her to be afraid. Giddy with shock, she realized that the hand was bleeding badly and she was in need of help. She turned the knob and saw the face of the caller through a blur.

"Good afternoon. I was on my way to the pueblo—" A man's voice began, then seeing her plight, changed tones completely. "What on earth happened to *you*? Down, Jane Doe, old girl. . . Oh, Kitty!"

Kitty felt herself being swept up into a pair of muscular arms in a way she had been held before. The embrace was warm and comfortable. It said that everything was going to be all right, and that it didn't matter at all that she looked like Mary Poppins or reeked of sardines. It only mattered that she was injured and in his arms. . . so familiar. . . as was his voice, Kitty realized just before passing out. *Clayton.* Clayton telling her to have no fear.

6

It seemed the most natural thing in the world to awaken and find herself relaxed against Clayton as Kitty floated in the pink haze of preconsciousness. She pulled away slightly to get a better view of his face—to make sure she wasn't dreaming. He stopped her motion with hard hands on her arms. The touch was electrifying. With a grateful sigh she sank back against him.

Gently but firmly he pushed her away. For Kitty it was as if icewater had been dashed in her face. It had seemed so innocent to her...but maybe Clayton felt that she had tried to move in on him. Well,

Mother had warned her, even as the stab of pain in her left hand was warning her now. She had almost no memory of his having bandaged the wound, but the work looked professional. Involuntarily she reached the injured hand toward him in gratitude. Then, remembering, she let it ease to the couch.

"I've been nothing but trouble, haven't I?"

"Women usually are!" Then his tone softened. "Do you feel like getting dressed? You need a tetanus shot."

"Oh, I must look a fright!" Kitty remembered the mess her hair had gotten itself into behind the old kerchief and the soot on her nose—and goodness knows what her clothes looked and smelled like!

Clayton groaned. "She decides to end it all by slashing her palms, is rescued by a gallant knight who restores her will to live—which may depend on a tetanus booster—but the lady is concerned with how she looks," Clayton spoke to some imaginary third person as he eased Kitty to her feet. His solemn face made the words comical.

Kitty giggled, then, feeling faint, leaned on Clayton's shoulder until the room righted itself. "Well, you've seen me at my worst both times, and I seem to have a talent for bringing out the worst in you... oh, not that I'm ungrateful. I'm glad you happened along, but I was a bother again."

"I came of my own accord," he reminded her. "So I guess your worst, as you phrase it, didn't scare me off. Now, get dressed!"

Clayton gave her a playful push toward the bathroom.

Showering was awkward because Kitty had

difficulty keeping her injured hand elevated. But she was grateful for the time because, under the soothing spray of warm water, she put together the composite of Clayton Madrone. She had mentioned his "worsts" with no mention of his "bests." He was not always the overcautious, suspicious, downright rude man any more than she was always the sooty ragamuffin. *Would one call him a man with a split personality?* Kitty wondered as she reached for a dry towel. "Fractured" would be more like it. He was a dozen men in one. He was probably a genius at writing, and consequently temperamental. Was it his writing he didn't want exposed, or was it his heart? He was so cautious, so on guard against being found out. And yet he had been gentle, kind, and (dare she think it?) *interested!* Something special had passed between them—something far greater than the "physical attraction" he had mentioned to Colette...not that the attraction wasn't there! Embarrassed at such thinking, Kitty toweled her hair vigorously.

After all, she had only met this man a short time ago. Getting acquainted took time. And this one was harder to know than most. "Not really," her reflection seemed to be contradicting as Kitty swept her cloud of hair up and secured it in a loose knot. "You're learning to understand him already—the part that nobody else knows exists."

It was true. His moods were as unpredictable as the desert thundershowers. But when one knew they were unpredictable, one expected sudden change. He was a constant surprise and no surprise at all. A writer. A doctor. A vet. A *preacher!* All of those parts, with the whole being greater than the sum of its parts. Kitty reached for her lip gloss and smiled into the mirror, aware for the first time of the dark shine of her hair. Maybe it had always shone. But the all-over glow was new—put there by a stranger. She would have to wait for him to declare himself. But until then he was her "beloved stranger"!

• • •

The little village, or pueblo to the local residents, appeared as suddenly as a mirage. Kitty was surprised at the greenery surrounding the dozen or so stores. "An oasis," Clayton explained.

"And no more than a mile or so from me. I'll be able to walk." Kitty looked with delight at the bouquet of buildings.

"No!" The word was so quickly spoken that it carried a note of alarm. Then, in a calmer voice, Clayton explained, "This is rattlesnake country, and the climate is deceptive. Because of the low humidity, people don't feel the heat." All of that was true, but Kitty had a feeling he wanted to add further caution. If there had been more time she might have told him of the strange night noises. Well, maybe on the way home . . . or she could invite him in for iced tea—

"The doctor's office," Clayton announced, pulling to the right to park beside a row of cottonwood trees. A few minutes later they were entering a small adobe building where a soft-spoken man—Indian, Kitty guessed—introduced himself as "Dr. Jim." He checked the hand capably, then gave her an injection.

"I would advise catching your own fish until this heals," he said without the trace of a smile.

Kitty thanked him, but when she asked what the charges were, the man only shook his head. "My Welcome Wagon gift," he surprised her by saying—again with no smile.

I like him, she thought. *Just as I like all the other men I have met here. Colette Drubay was probably a poor example of the women*, she mused as they went out into the blinding sunlight.

"Well, do we buy fishing gear and follow the doctor's orders or go straight home?" Clayton asked.

"I doubt if he'd want me to sit on my hands," Kitty said lightly, "but I do need to check on Jane Doe—" She was about to suggest the iced tea when her eyes came to rest on a sign that stopped her in midsentence: GOTSCHALK & GOTSCHALK.

She pointed to the sign in surprise.

"I had no idea they would be out here. How in the world could they hope for any clientele?"

"Oh, they have no problem, believe me!" Clayton spoke calmly enough, but there was a note of disapproval in his words. "They handle Indian affairs, and I'm sure you know they handle real estate."

"I didn't know."

Clayton shrugged. "It's unimportant, as far as you're concerned, I suppose. But didn't you know about their handling the contracts with the film producers?"

"I didn't know that either."

"That *is* important."

"I don't understand, but there are some other questions I have—that is, if I won't detain you."

By way of answer, Clayton placed a steadying hand on her arm and they walked the few paces

to the weathered building. "There are some errands
I need to do. This is the bank, and you'll see a small
grocery store on the left. It's not exactly a modern
shopping center, but it holds us over until we get
to the city."

"I like it," Kitty said. "It's rustic and quaint—
like a real frontier trading post. The cobblestone
streets and old saloon signs give it a ghost-town
look."

They had reached the door leading to the attorneys' office. "That's the general idea, of course, since
the place is used as a setting for a good many movies.
Take your time, Kitty. Ask all the questions you
need to, especially about your father and any arrangement for filming."

Kitty found the advice odd, especially when the
junior partner himself had cautioned her against taking anything for granted, jumping into anything too
quickly, and trusting other people. Obviously Rhett
worried about her. About the "strange happenings,"
too. But why had he not told her more—or less? And,
as an attorney, he should tell her about the contracts.
Wasn't that his business? Mr. Gotschalk had said
Rhett looked after her father's ranch. *For how long?*
She wondered.

Realizing that Clayton had gone into a place
marked PHARMACY, Kitty knocked on the door
marked GOTSCHALK & GOTSCHALK. There was
no answer, but she felt that one of the men must
be in the office because the large black car that the
senior Mr. Gotschalk had driven to the "Circle Left"
was parked beside the building. Its shining sleekness
looked out of place in this quaint village, where the
only thing needed for a Western movie was a gang
of bandits and a tumbleweed rolling past.

When there was no answer the second time she knocked, Kitty took hold of the doorknob and turned it experimentally. As she suspected, the door was unlocked. But the tiny cubicle serving as a reception room was deserted.

Good manners dictated that she sit down and wait. But the room was stuffy and hot. Her hand was beginning to throb. And, for some reason, she felt irritated. The Kitty Fairfield of a week ago would have tiptoed out, but the Kitty Fairfield of today knocked on the door marked "Private."

Mr. Gotschalk, even grayer than she remembered, opened the door. Peering from behind his large rimless glasses, he reminded Kitty of an owl awakened from his nap. "Oh—Oh, it's you, Miss Fairfield!" He ran a nervous, white hand through his thin hair. "I'm glad you've come, as I need to give you a progress report."

Kitty took the chair he pulled out. A layer of dust covered it, giving her the feeling that it had not been occupied for some time. What a mess her navy cotton skirt would be! Oh, well, Clayton was used to seeing her at her worst. All she needed now was a dust devil to dance through the open window and play havoc with her hair.

Opening her bag, she removed her list and waited for Mr. Gotschalk's report before asking questions. He studied the papers in front of him, pursing his lips in concentration. When at last he spoke it was as if he were trying to convince himself before expecting her to believe his words.

"I don't know how this happened—I just don't know. But it seems you have no half-brother. The fact is that you have no siblings at all." Mr. Gotschalk rose from his chair, mopped his brow with the back of his hand, and turned a small electric fan more directly toward himself. "What you *do* have is a *stepbrother*. The first Mrs. Fairfield had been married previously. We were unable to find the name—which is of no consequence anyway, is it?"

"None that I can think of," Kitty said slowly, wondering why he had asked her. "What you're telling me then is that there are no other heirs. And that the 'Circle Left' is mine."

"That is correct—at least in part. You see, there is a mortgage, interest due—let's see, yes, that's correct, June first."

Two weeks! There was no way she could meet the payment. The man should know that. *He did know it*, Kitty found herself thinking as their eyes met. He knew and he seemed almost pleased. The thought provoked from her the most impetuous words of her life. "I'll take care of it."

She was sure he all but toppled from the stiff-backed chair in which he sat, so great was his surprise. "Very well," he said slowly, "if you are sure you want to keep the property."

"You said yourself that it was well worth redeeming when we spoke on the telephone."

"So I did, Miss Fairfield, but that was before I knew another buyer was looking at the property. He made a good offer—"

"Who?"

"I'm sorry, but I am unable to reveal the name of my client. I can only say that he made a good offer. Very good."

Kitty leaned forward. "Is the potential buyer connected with the film producers who have used the ranch as a setting?"

The lawyer, who had remained standing since adjusting the fan, sat down heavily. "No—not that I am aware of. I—you see, Miss Fairfield—Miss Fairfield—Kitty, this is most embarrassing, but I was unaware of that arrangement until recently. Mr. Dawson will be better able to answer your questions."

Kitty, having had no business experience, marveled at her ability to have kept ahead in the conversation. "If there is a contractual agreement involving money, where did the payments go? Why weren't they applied to the taxes?"

"Mr. Dawson will have some explanation, I am sure. It is unfortunate he's out—out your way, come to think of it, caring for the horses—"

"How many are there?"

"Here again, I am unable to say. Your father made mention of the horses but came up with no number of head. I'd think the number would vary according to need—riding horses and sometimes a need for what appeared to be a herd in the making of the films. Are you beginning to get the picture?"

"In a sense," Kitty answered. *And in another I'm not*, she thought, because every question answered meant new ones unanswered. One mystery wrapped in another and another.

Kitty checked the list of questions in her hand. Most had been answered—at least, for the time being. She was relieved to learn that Rhett, making use of the information she had furnished, was in the process of getting duplicates made of her I.D. cards—some of the forms needing her signature. Kitty signed, inquired how to obtain a temporary driver's permit, and was about to go when she recalled one question she had left unanswered.

"By the way, the 'Circle Left' is not for sale," she said.

The drive home was pleasant—so pleasant that Kitty decided against telling Clayton about the disturbing noises. In her cleaning she had found several padlocks that were in working order. She would put one on both the front and the back doors. The window latches worked and the piles of newspapers and magazines would meet the need for the remaining precaution she planned. Grandmother Cramer always insisted that there be crumpled papers piled beneath the windows. Being a light sleeper, she would awaken if an intruder stepped on the paper, she said. Kitty had thought it was amusing at the time. Now she thought it might be wise.

The conversation went other-directional anyway. Clayton insisted that she visit most of the shops. "Even is you need nothing today, you may later," he said. And then he surprised her by adding, "And I wanted to introduce you around."

The shop fronts were deceptive. The interior decorating and the merchandise in most cases was up-to-date, in contrast to the rustic appearances of the exterior of the buildings. In the shop boasting HARDWARE, Kitty purchased a gallon of seafoam paint at half price. "Last year's color," the proprietor explained the discount. It would do wonders for the kitchen, but how much did she dare spend?

The matter was decided when Clayton caught her eye and nodded approval. Green must be his favorite color, she thought, remembering the shades of it he had spread about his own house. And two of the dressing gowns had been green. The thought of other women having worn the garments twisted at her heart.

Feeling color stain her face and not wanting Clayton to take note, Kitty turned her back and busied herself endorsing a traveler's check. The cashier, to her relief, asked for no identification. And, with Clayton swinging the bucket in one hand and holding her arm with the other, they walked out and toward the sign boasting DRY GOODS. *From all appearances*, Kitty found herself thinking, *we could be a young married couple in the village for the week's supplies.*

To her delight, there was a remnant of gauzy fabric which Kitty was sure would be large enough for kitchen curtains. And the shade was almost identical to the paint. She was thinking that there might be enough material in the extra bedspread to make living room drapes when Clayton said suddenly, "You sew, I see. Would you like to use the little portable machine Jana—my sister—left?"

Kitty turned shining eyes to him. "Oh, I'd love that! If you're sure it's all right—"

Clayton laughed. "I'm sure! I can assure you that all talents in stitchery lie with Jana. But I'm the better cook—speaking of which, how would you like a whopping big ice cream soda, the old-fashioned kind?"

It was as if they had known each other forever as they sipped their sodas, laughing at the size of the glasses and each wagering that the other could not finish.

Somehow it pleased Kitty that she finished first, announcing her victory with the sucked-in sound of air in her empty straw. And it pleased her too that Clayton thought her capable of doing something right—even if it was only using a sewing machine. She was glad he *didn't* think of her as a spy!

"Wipe your mouth. You've got a pink mustache." Clayton handed her his paper napkin.

Kitty wiped her mouth. "Easier for me than you," she laughed.

"I've been thinking of shaving mine. What do you think?"

"I think," Kitty said, suddenly sobering, "that it's up to you."

Clayton did not answer, but he looked at her strangely, as if she had said something wrong. She hoped not. With a sudden feeling that she must snatch quickly at happiness, Kitty was determined that their day together would be marred by nothing—not even the gnawing suspicion that Clayton was in love with someone else. Kitty reached across the table and touched his hand. "I wanted to tell you that I'm enjoying the morning program you do—even though I don't always understand—"

His large hand covered hers gently. "That's the whole idea," he said, his eyes burning with intensity. "I try to speak to the new converts among the Indians in a language they can understand—using the things of nature with which they commune— and at the same time not talking down to other Christians."

Kitty drew a long breath. Something in his sincerity had touched her deeply. It was more than a touch of two hands. It was a touch of two hearts—and in a realm that she had not experienced before. She hoped he would say more, but he seemed to be waiting for her.

"I'm afraid I don't fall in either class, Clay...I mean...like I told you that first night, I'm a nothing."

His hand tightened. "Don't say that," he whispered. "Don't ever say that again. You're very special in God's eyes—and in mine."

Kitty felt herself drawn into a bright circle of love—Clayton's and God's. But the circle needed to be filled in, made solid. A circumference was not enough to satisfy her inner hunger. "Tell me more, Clay. Make me understand."

The words were no more than a whisper. But Clay heard. And Kitty had a feeling that God heard, too. What followed was the most beautiful experience of her life.

Clayton continued to hold Kitty's hand as he

talked. His grasp, like his voice, was gentle. Even with the hum of voices around them, she felt the same reverence she remembered in the few visits to Sunday school with neighboring children. Something strange and wonderful had happened when teachers held up pictures of angels guarding children as they slept and Jesus, the Good Shepherd, cradling a baby lamb in loving arms. But Grandmother and Mother seemed unimpressed when Kitty shared the feeling she had experienced. And so, eventually, she put Jesus, the loving Savior, away with Santa Claus, the Easter Bunny, and the Tooth Fairy, labeling them childhood fantasies. Until today! Until she heard Clay's simple words.

"It's too bad you never knew your father, Kitten. I knew him only slightly—enough to feel that he was a loving man, much like me in many ways—"

What happened, Clay? What happened to my father? And to you? Tell me...I need to know... but when Kitty turned quizzical eyes to Clayton, he put a silencing finger to his lips and went on.

"You see, I think fathers give us a little taste of God's love for His children. There's a story in the book of Luke that tells of a son who left home, broke all the rules and his father's heart, and then came home. The beautiful message is that the father saw him when he was 'yet a great way off' and ran— not walked, mind you, *ran*—to meet the boy. I can almost feel the bear hug of welcome! The father forgave him, and it's my guess that the prodigal son never again was the wayward son. Who wouldn't choose the good life of compassion, love, forgiveness, and understanding?"

"Is that the way it is with God, Clay?"

Clayton's grip on her hands tightened. He was holding both now, causing little flames of fire to dart through the injured hand. But it didn't matter. "That's how it is."

Inside Kitty, the cocoon of doubts, fears, and dark imaginings unwound to release the shining butterfly of joy. The circle was filled in, converted into a firm foundation for her newborn spirit to rest upon. Today. Tomorrow. And on through the years.

"An eternity of love." The words tasted sweeter than the soda to her tongue.

"An eternity of love," Clayton repeated after her, paying no attention when the waitress brought his check. "And do you know what the father did to convince his son of that?" When Kitty shook her head, Clayton said softly, "Luke writes that he 'fell on his neck and kissed him!' "

With those words, Clayton eased his long frame from the chair to standing position, leaned across the table, and kissed her once on each cheek. "Like this!" he said.

His behavior did not surprise Kitty half as much as her own. She, the undemonstrative one, rose and, standing on tiptoe, kissed Clayton's lips. The kiss was brief. Gentle. Like a private breeze that nobody else feels. But there was response in Clayton's eyes. The shining promise of love! Kitty knew then that she had seen the real man behind the beard—in the flesh and in the spirit.

This was a day to drink in deeply. Kitty longed to stretch it out. Make it last forever—spanning the distance between the "earthly here" and the "heavenly there" that Clayton described as they returned to the car beneath the cottonwood trees, now golden with the last rays of the setting sun. But they *must* get back. What would poor Jane Doe be thinking? Yes, they must go. Quickening her steps in an effort to match Clayton's long stride, Kitty almost danced with elation.

Cares of the days having faded, she was reluctant to tell Clayton what she had and had not found out in Mr. Gotschalk's office. And certainly, after all of Clayton's reassurances, this was no time to bring up the matter of her fears. And so, lulled by the humming rhythm of the tires as they drove home, Kitty relaxed against the back of the seat beside the man who was no longer an enemy, a hermit, or even her beloved stranger. This was. . .the man she planned to marry.

Would he propose? How should a girl let her feelings be made known without being aggressive? For a man who had been hurt, she had a feeling it would take a long time to resurrect Clayton's faith in the opposite sex. . .but the time would come. . . *later, later, later*, the tires hummed. She could wait.

The car slowed. They were nearing home. It was good to be home, and already Kitty's mind had awakened to tomorrow, when she would begin refurbishing. But her heart had overslept. It was still dealing with today and all the joy it had brought—wondering when she would see Clayton again. And, when they met, if he would be *her* Clayton or the secret part of him that belonged to somebody else.

As Clayton applied the brake, he said without preamble, "Would you like to attend church with me Sunday?"

"I'd love to!" Kitty remembered with delight how

the church, although it was small, seemed to tower up, sunlit and airy. It had, she thought at the time, a singing quality as if the bell, even in its stillness, begged for human voices. And then, as if sensing there would be no accompaniment, it spoke. The walls around it caught the sound of it—as did Kitty's heart. "Yes," she repeated, "I'd love to." Something stirred in her memory then, a verse that the long-ago Sunday school teacher had repeated in each class: " 'I was glad when they said unto me, Let us go into the house of the Lord.' " Almost unthinking, Kitty recited the words aloud.

"What!" Clayton's word was more exclamation than question. And then he laughed. "You know, we are going to be a constant surprise to each other. Kitten—"

Kitty held her breath at the tremor in his voice. But the moment was lost in the lumbering crash of Jane Doe's bloated body trying to dodge bushes and greet them with excited barks.

Jane Doe! Somebody has let her out. Who has been inside?

8

Kitty awakened more refreshed than she had
been since her arrival. She looked forward to a
busy day of painting. Clayton had made no mention as to when he would bring the sewing machine.
Soon, she hoped. It would be nice to show him
on Sunday, which ended her first week of desert
living, that she had converted a house into a home.
Admittedly, she wanted to please him. Oh, she
wanted that very much! And staying busy would
keep her mind from the greater problems that
lay ahead. . .or behind—especially the intruder.

I should have talked with Clayton about the

mortgage, Kitty thought as she prepared a hasty breakfast for herself and Jane Doe. She had not wanted to bother him with her personal problems, make him feel she was asking for a loan. Hadn't she been trouble enough? Yet it was he who had mentioned the motion picture contracts. Well, she would tell him the outcome as soon as there was a chance to talk with Rhett.

At the thought of Rhett, Kitty stopped pouring out the dry dog food in Jane Doe's dish. Didn't Mr. Gotschalk say Rhett had planned to come to the "Circle Left" yesterday? As far as she knew, she had the only key to the house. And it would be trespassing for anyone, even her attorney, to enter without her permission now that the place was occupied by the person who soon would become its rightful owner. So it was unfair for her to suspect that it was he who let the dog out—wasn't it?

Jane Doe rubbed her finely chiseled head against Kitty's thigh, her great eyes saying, "Please." Kitty patted the gray nose absentmindedly and finished pouring the morning ration. "Courageous and loyal, lots of intelligence so responds well to training" was how the keeper had described the breed. Kitty was thankful indeed for the animal's presence.

As she busied herself with tidying up after coffee and toast, Kitty tried to concentrate on the projects she had planned. But somewhere deep down inside her the nagging suspicion remained that Rhett had been inside the house even though it made no sense. What could he be looking for?

Determined to shake away such thinking, Kitty began hastily collecting the wadded papers she had placed beneath the windows last night. She had padlocked the doors. Then, to condition herself against fear, she had checked out Clayton's radio-message passages in the Bible he had included in the books he sent along with her. "I was with you in weakness, and in fear, and in much trembling." She read the verse, then repeated it aloud from 1 Corinthians 2:3. *God was all-knowing, so He must have known that someday I would need those words when He whispered them to Paul.* Though in past tense, the ancient words spoke directly to her—saying that she too must leave her fears behind. Give them to the Lord. Make them her past tense.

Closing the Bible, Kitty turned out the light and lay wondering how one began a prayer. "Hello, Lord. This is Your prodigal daughter—coming home—seeking forgiveness. I'm not very good at talking. I listen better. So why don't You just speak to me—tell me what You want me to do and to be? I want to love and be loved. I guess that's all I ever needed."

There ought to be more to say, but somehow she believed that God understood. It was almost as if His Presence filled the room. And, to her surprise, no additional words were needed.

Jane Doe gave a little sigh of contentment. Kitty stretched her full length, tensed, and relaxed. Then both of them slept the night through. . . .

And now this morning she was ready to roll up her sleeves and transform this house as God was transforming her life. She felt young, alert, alive— her body rippling with spiritual muscle it had not had before. Why, there was hardly any soreness left in her hand as she stirred the paint!

Kitty applied a sample of the paint to a stick as the clerk at the hardware store had shown her and found it to her liking. *Seafoam green is a proper name*, she thought as she looked down at the wide path of new life left by the roller. By 8:30 A.M. the kitchen was a welcome oasis, the underwater green of walls and ceiling inviting and cool.

It was time to tune in for Clayton's voice. Laying the roller aside, Kitty went into the bedroom to switch on the program. As she passed the paint bucket, she was surprised to see how far the paint was going. Having a rubber base, it could be diluted with water, according to directions. At least she would be able to paint the bedroom and bath. The spare room could be left for awhile. As far as she could tell, it housed only an old trunk, a rollaway bed, and stacks of boxes—typical, she supposed of a man living alone. She remembered Clayton's cluttered desk and smiled. Then she concentrated on the organ music which filled the room.

"Good morning! God loves you. Before I begin this day's short message, I ask you to look closely at the beautiful world around you and think, 'This is what God created with His own hands—because He loves me.' " Clayton's voice, pitched to a low, conversational tone, paused to allow listeners the moment's meditation. Then he continued: "This world is your playground. Yours to enjoy. Yours to protect. But there is more to faith than striving for heaven. This world, your playground, is also God's workshop! There is work to do before we join Him in heaven. The law of God is the way of life, His kingdom. It is not enough to be filled with joy. We must share that joy with others. That is our work! Why should we work for the One who loves us? Because we love *Him*! Say it. Then say it again. 'God loves me and I love Him.' How many times? Until you know it is true. And now I leave with you this message straight from His Book: 'There is no fear in love....' "

Kitty did not hear Clayton's last few words. She was busy with a prayer. "Thank You, Lord," she whispered. "Thank You for answering my last night's question. I love You!"

God chooses His workers well, Kitty thought as she guided the roller, skillfully now, up and down the bedroom walls. Clayton was eloquent. She wondered for the first time where his sermonettes originated. Surely not from the pueblo. She wondered, too, what his books were like. Today, she resolved, she would examine some of them.

The painting went well. Now and then Kitty turned to watch the long green tongues of color follow her roller strokes like a shadow—a shadow more beautiful then the object that cast it. *And that*, she thought, *is what God must have done with Clayton.*

At noon, the bedroom finished, Kitty made herself a sandwich and poured fresh water for Jane Doe. Usually the dog, as if to show appreciation, took a few obliging laps. Today she lay still, her eyes closed. The change concerned Kitty. She wondered just how close at hand this "whelping" (wasn't that what Clayton called it?) was. She shuddered. She had never witnessed birth and would be no help in case Jane Doe had trouble. She must consult Clayton. He knew about such things. Kitty checked the telephone to make sure it was in working order; then, taking her sandwich, she lay down across the bed and picked up the first book from the stack that Clayton had given her.

When first she began reading, Kitty nibbled away at her sandwich. Then she became so absorbed in the book that she laid her unfinished sandwich on the bedside table alongside her father's scribbled notes.

Clayton Madrone Senior, Clay's father, had been a minister all his adult life, the preface told her. "Conversion to Christianity came naturally to me," the publisher quoted the younger Clayton as saying. "And since my father did most of his preaching on Indian reservations, it seemed equally natural that I would grow to love and understand his people. The Indians' love for the things of nature made it 'only natural' that I would seek a way to combine these backgrounds and come up with what some reviewers have termed my nature sermons."

Young Clayton wanted to minister in some manner other than the pulpit. After graduating from a Bible college in the East, he accepted an invitation to conduct short services to urban listeners by way of radio. His short, punchy messages caught on "as a convenience for those who wanted to get it over with and play golf in the afternoon." That quote brought to Kitty a picture of Clay's slow, rewarding smile, followed by a low laugh when he said the words.

She read on. The programs were so well-accepted that a larger radio station asked him to conduct a half-hour talk show, then extended it to an hour, then offered a contract for a simulcast combining radio and television which Clayton would host. Kitty gasped as she read of its successes and the offers which followed the program—offers from well-known evangelists. And then from the film-making industry. No wonder he expected to be recognized! The name was unfamiliar, but she might have recognized his face, Kitty thought ruefully, if he hadn't hidden it behind that heavy growth of beard.

Maybe he would explain that, too. But there was no mention of his private life. One got a glimpse of the true Clayton Madrone, however, through reading his admission of a lack of fulfillment in the light-action-camera life which the radio-television programs demanded. "They called it a *show*, and that's exactly what it was—a show. I had lost contact with the two kingdoms I loved—the animal kingdom and the kingdom of God! Something had to be done."

It was then that Clayton's father became ill here on this Arizona ranch, the "Circle Right." To his surprise, the older man had found his own unique way of reaching out to others, even in his illness. In what had been a guest bedroom, Mr. Madrone had set up the beginnings of the completely equipped office that Clayton had now. "So from rags to riches, the quarters are now equipped with electronic machinery for producing a one-man electronic ministry in the seclusion of my home." The tapes, once serving only one low-wattage station during his father's time, were now distributed to 20 larger radio stations throughout the country. "I will always be thankful for that father-son relationship. . . ." Kitty could almost hear the catch in Clayton's voice as he said those words, and could almost see the prodigal-son glow she had seen in his eyes.

But why had he become such a recluse? Kitty

read on but could find no direct answer. There was mention of one sister. That would be Jana. But Clayton said nothing of his mother. Neither did he provide a clue to his lifestyle—unless one could use his claim that he could reach more listeners on one tape than churches could reach in months, maybe years. "My job is to get the Word of the Lord to all persons—including the shut-ins, either on tape or in typewritten copy. I honor each request and am especially happy when the physical or the spiritual cripple asks for help, because I am a firm believer that it is in acknowledging our weakness that we are made strong!" All this took time. Kitty could see now that Clayton truly needed solitude in order to carry on his work. He needed money, too. The preface made no mention of finances. She wondered about that. . .but, most of all, she wondered how this strong man, so all-powerful in everything he undertook, could have allowed his heart to become so victimized.

Kitty rose from her cramped position and, without finishing her sandwich, began to paint the bathroom. When there was only one wall to finish, the paint ran low. She added water and stirred. Expecting the color to dilute, Kitty was pleased to see that even the most discerning eye would be unable to see the difference. It was just a minor thing, but it made her feel better—as if she were learning to manage her life.

It was now too late to tackle another major job, Kitty decided. So, after a cool lemonade and a promise to take Jane Doe for a sunset walk, she showered. There had been no response from Jane Doe, but Clayton had said some lethargy was natural. *Natural.* He leaned heavily on that word. Thinking of Clayton, the man, eventually led to thought of Clayton, the writer. How could they be one and the same?

Kitty checked on a small pot roast she had cooking in an enormous Dutch-oven utensil she had found. The roast was browning perfectly, its spicy odor filling the rooms as if inviting company. It was good to be alone, she thought. Good to test herself. To prove herself *to* herself. But what then? After she learned to "love herself" (and if she understood the Bible right, she was expected to do that), it seemed to her that one was supposed to expand... to love God...to love *others*! Of course, "Love thy neighbor" presented some problems! Kitty grinned with her newfound sense of humor. She would have to consult God on this matter. Just which one did He mean—the one to the right or the one to the left?

Jane Doe, as far as Kitty could tell, had not moved. The afternoon sun was just beginning to cool. It was still too warm for walking, so Kitty sat down and opened Clayton's book again.

Clayton himself wrote a short foreword explaining some of the fears and superstitions which had come down through the earlier tribes. "What the first Americans did not understand they attempted to explain by legend—how the sky came to be blue, how the grass came to be green, and why the rabbit has long ears. But the one thing they could not explain was the thinking of their many gods. Not understanding the gods, they lived in constant fear of angering them. And, sadly, the Indian has never been able to tell his own story. He had no writing. His history passed down by word of mouth from father to son and became part truth and part myth. But this we know: The first inhabitants of the New World loved nature. . . ."

The book, Kitty discovered, contained a collection of short devotional thoughts—thoughts so fresh, strong, unified, and sincere that they should earn the author a secure place in literature. "How beautiful, Lord, how beautiful!" she breathed over and over as she read of God's hanging the sun, moon, and stars in place, then adding wind to divide the land and water. All of this was to manifest God's goodness and glory and His love for man, who had dominion over all other creatures. "Let us love God with all our hearts and praise all of nature as a work of His hands! It is He who gave us the Earth to sustain us, producing the rich, ripe fruits, colored flowers, and herbs. It is He who made everything beautiful and gave it to us, asking only that we love Him—and love one another. It is He who is ever with us in time of fear. For He does not hide His face. . . ."

Oh, Clayton, then why have you hidden yours? Her heart cried.

9

Clayton brought the sewing machine the next morning. Kitty was polishing a silver urn she had found near the fireplace. To her dismay, the urn was filled with kindling. It was beautifully engraved and would make a good conversation piece for the dining room window just above the table.

At the sound of the car door slamming, Jane Doe wagged her white-tipped tail but made no move to rise. "You're some watchdog, pal!" Kitty teased her. "Or maybe it's a friend?"

Wiping her hands quickly, Kitty went to the living room and peeked through a slit in the worn drapes. Her heart gave a double beat at the sight of Clayton's lithe body moving noiselessly up the walk, machine in hand. It seemed incredulous that a man of his size could step so lightly on gravel that there was not a sound. But, thank goodness, she thought with a smile, she was scrubbed and clean today, in spite of a restless night.

Happily she opened the door and gave Clayton a welcoming smile. "Oh, Clayton, hi! I'm so glad to get the machine—come in—and what's in the sack?" she said with a quick rush of words as he handed her a paper bag.

"Coffee cake," Clayton's smile was the one she had grown to appreciate because it was so seldom. But when it came, it cleared the air like a sudden shower. "I told you I was the cook. How are you at coffee?"

"I confess to using the instant kind. But not today, I guess. I see you've brought your own. You don't take chances, do you?"

Immediately she regretted the words. To cover her confusion, she bent over the sack, poking at something small and green that looked at first like a bouquet. "Fern? I loved the one at your house—"

"I saw you admiring it and potted you one. Where's the measuring spoon? I don't trust you with the percolator. Can you slice the cake without cutting yourself again?"

"Clayton, be nice!"

And suddenly they were laughing. The day, already bright, grew brighter. Encased in the seafoam bubble she had painted, they were floating, free of gravity, in an ocean of sunlight... just the two of them in a newly created galaxy.

Truly the Lord was making His face shine upon them!

Clayton finished measuring the coffee and turned to her. "How is the hand, by the way?"

His words brought the bubble closer to earth, but Kitty's voice sounded far away in her own ears when she said her hand was fine. *Everything's fine. Everything's wonderful!*

"Let me have a look."

Kitty laid down the serrated knife she was using to cut the coffee cake. "See—I only have a Band-Aid on it."

Clayton took her hand, examined it, and then said, "What's wrong, Kitten? You're trembling. And you look haggard. You've been working too hard, but you've done wonders with this place. Your father would be proud of you."

Acutely aware that he still held her hand, Kitty tried to speak in a natural voice. "It's nothing— I—I didn't sleep very well. I kept hearing noises—"

Clayton's body seemed to stiffen. "What sort of noises?"

"It was nothing, I'm sure—just the creaks and groans of an old house," she tried to amend.

"This house is neither old enough to creak and groan nor is there anything wrong with it congenitally," Clayton answered. "Why didn't you call me?"

Oh, she would have if there had been any emergency...but one could hardly call the sound of footsteps outside her window—*if* that's what it was—then, suddenly, Kitty found herself telling Clayton all about the sounds. "Some of the noises could have been my imagination," she ended, "but then last night, I saw him—at least, I think it was a man. I'm certain it was the outline of a person. But," she frowned, "the peculiar thing was that he—this person—didn't try to hide. It was more like *wanting* to be seen. And that scared me worst of all."

Clayton stroked her hand, frowning darkly in concentration. "Did you turn on a light or try to investigate?"

Kitty shuddered. "Goodness, no! I hid behind the curtains until the intruder ran when Jane Doe began to bark."

"You acted wisely. The prowler could have been trying to coax you from the house, you know."

"I didn't think of that," Kitty admitted, "but who would want to harm me? Everyone's been so nice—"

"Have you talked with the Colonel?"

Instinctively Kitty withdrew her hand and raised it to her lips, biting on a forefinger in her shock. "You don't think he's dangerous, do you, Clay? I thought you said—isn't he supposed to be a nice old English gentleman?"

Clayton reached out and put his arms around her in a loose, protective embrace. "There now, I've frightened you. I take it you *haven't* met Colonel Witham—and, yes, I *did* say he's a fine man. I meant that he will be a means of protection if you intend to stay—and you *do*, don't you?" His embrace tightened just as the percolator boiled over. Clayton ran to retrieve it from the burner, and what might have been an intimate moment exploded in shared laughter. Kitty recovered first.

"I thought you could operate one of those things."

"Mine's electric," he defended, lifting the pot as

if to weigh it. "Where are the cups? I hope there's a pint left!"

"If not, here are a couple of straws. We'll share," Kitty answered lightly, handing him the only two mugs she could find that matched. When their hands touched, each drew back.

Seconds later they were enjoying the freshly brewed coffee and chatting companionably. Kitty brought Clayton up-to-date on Jane Doe's symptoms. His comments were reassuring. They talked about his books. Actually, Kitty talked and Clayton said little. But she could tell by the warm glow in his eyes that her words of appreciation pleased him.

"So much work," she said. "Doesn't anybody help you?"

"A cleaning lady comes once a week. But nobody helps with the writing—" Clayton paused as if looking for some signal in her eyes. "I'm thinking, though, that anybody who can operate a sewing machine should be able to operate a typewriter."

Kitty caught her breath. "You mean—*me*?"

Clayton looked about the kitchen. "We seem to be alone."

She would have to look for work to survive. But working with Clayton presented two problems. If she took on the responsibility of helping with his writing, it would put the two of them in closer contact than was safe. Too, it surprised her to feel that anything done for the Lord should be a gift.

"Well?" Clayton's voice cut into her thoughts.

Not sure how to put her feelings into words, Kitty stalled. "Can't you type?" she asked at last.

Clayton's laugh surprised her. "Oh, you're something, Kitten Eyes! You really are. You speak of

my work overload, then imply that I should possess
my own set of skills. The Indians call that 'speaking with forked tongue'! But to answer your question, my typing is done with my two index fingers.
Works about as well as my two thumbs did with
the coffeepot."

"I'm out of practice—it's been a long time—" Kitty
began, then with a new determination said simply,
"Yes, I will type for you."

"Good!" Clayton sounded genuinely pleased. "I
will bring over the material from time to time. Just
let me know when you are ready."

He would bring it over. That should have simplified
things for her. Instead, Kitty felt a keen sense of
disappointment. Not that she preferred to work in
his house, or even felt that it was wise. Her disappointment came from his chin-up, shoulders-back,
chest-out manner—intended, she felt with a blush
of embarrassment, to maintain a proper psychological and physical distance.

The moment passed quickly. Clayton offered to
show her the attachments to the machine, admitting that he did not know their names or functions.
That set her laughing again.

"But you can help me hang the urn," she said. "I
want to put in the fern you brought and place it here
by the window."

During the process of locating a hammer, nails,
and hook, then hanging the pot and adding the
plant, Kitty asked more about her father. "Do you
realize," she said, steadying the urn as Clayton
hammered, "that I've been here almost a week and
all I know about him is that we look a little alike
and he kept his radio tuned to a religious station?"

Clayton backed away to survey the hanging pot.

"A compliment to us both. We either have to lower this thing or take it down and clean the bottom of your hanging garden."

He was right. Kitty realized that she had forgotten the bottom. Even a casual observer would see that it was still tarnished, spoiling the otherwise-special touch she had hoped for. She nodded and Clayton removed the fern-filled urn. "Bring the polish. I'll do this one. There's an inscription here—"

As he scrubbed, Kitty looked eagerly over his shoulder, hoping that the inscribed words would reveal that the urn belonged to her—that it had been her father's all along instead of something he had picked up at an auction.

"What does it say? *Tell* me!" Over and over Kitty asked, crowding against him closer all the while in an effort to get a glimpse of the inscription. "What is that date?"

"June 1, 1960," he read and continued scrubbing. "Mean anything?"

"It was their wedding day!" Kitty said in awe. "Oh, Clay, do you realize this is like you're rubbing Aladdin's magic lamp while I wish for more insight into my past?"

Busy with the urn, Clayton did not reply. "You see," Kitty went on, "the inscription shows that the silver piece belonged to my parents...the only other community property being me, I guess. He was married before, you know—my father. I was afraid the urn belonged to her—"

"And should have gone to her son?"

"You knew I had a stepbrother, Clay? What was he like—and where is he now?"

Kitty had only a side view of Clayton's face. It

looked as if he had said more than he intended.
"I knew he existed. No more. Let it alone, Kitten,
all of it. I've found that delving into the past leads
to trouble, and neither of us needs any more of
that." He stopped rubbing and concentrated in
an effort to make out the lettering on the bottom
of the urn.

"What's his name, Clayton?" Kitty persisted.

He ignored her question. "I thought you were
interested in the inscription. I think I can make
it out now." He read the words slowly: "THROUGH
THE YEARS—WITH YOU!"

Clayton held the urn upside-down so Kitty could
reread the words. Unexpectedly, her eyes filled with
tears.

"Oh, Clayton, they must have expected their love
to go on forever. And look what happened. They
spent all those years alone—without each other.
Why, why would they have let something tear them
apart...make them bitter?"

Her tears spilled over then. With a pantherlike
leap he was at her side, putting protective arms
around her. Then pulling her close. Too close. Kitty
knew it was expected that she push him away...
protest...maybe laugh. But none of the reactions
would come. She found herself staring up into
his eyes, wondering if her own were as huge and
dark.

There was still time, she thought, as his head bent
in slow motion, his lips parting in silent request. Instead she lifted her face to him, closing her eyes, and
waiting for the inevitable kiss. This was where she
belonged. His arms were the haven she had hoped
for all her life.

But the kiss never came. Clayton pushed her

gently but firmly away. Kitty stared at him in wordless surprise. What could have happened to make him close the door of his heart and bolt it as well?

Kitty found herself murmuring something incoherent—thanking him for holding her—

"We all need to be held sometimes." Clayton stood like a statue and his voice was expressionless. "It hurts when we go back to childhood."

Closed as it was, his face looked vulnerable, hurt, lonely, and perplexed—as if he were trying to understand. It was another face to put into her composite. One to love and cherish. How could she reconcile all the faces of Clayton Madrone?

Deliberately she turned back to the urn. THROUGH THE YEARS . . . Kitty knew then that she could not go through life without him.

10

The drapes looked almost professional, Kitty
decided, as she backed away from the living room
windows to survey her tailoring job. There had
been a bad moment when it looked as if she might
run short of material; but, because the bedspread
was king-size (typical of a man's shopping, she
thought with a smile, considering the regular
size of the mattress), she managed to finish the
project—with one minor flaw. But who was going
to know that the corner pinch-pleat was smaller
than the others? The cauliflower color of the sum-
mer-weight cotton let in more sun than the tattered

purplish ones. The only name she could think of for the color was *eggplant*, the one vegetable she disliked! Thinking of the eggplant reminded her of the shape of Mr. Gotschalk's head. As she measured and basted the sheer material for the kitchen cafe curtains, Kitty wondered for the first time why nobody had mentioned the man's son. She put the thought aside as the curtains took shape.

Thanks to the aid of Clayton's sewing machine, the curtains were finished in no time, it seemed. She was in the process of looking for a screw that fell to the floor as the old curtains came down when there was a timid knock on the front door. It was totally unlike Clayton's knock, and not what she would expect of Rhett's.

Jane Doe tried to lift her heavy body, then—discouraged with its weight—sank back onto the rag rug. She sniffed, then closed her eyes. Well, that was something to go on, Kitty decided. Dogs were supposed to be sensitive to danger, and apparently Jane Doe did not think the caller was worth the effort a bark would take.

Kitty tried to see the door from the window, but rocks jutted out to cut off side vision. She opened the door just a crack.

"Yes?" she said cautiously and then was taken aback by the appearance of the rotund man who stood before her. *How could anyone tolerate corduroys and a thick, turtleneck sweater on such a warm morning?* was her first thought. Her second thought was that there was something apologetic and old-world about him. There was a certain elegance in the stance, a little like an aged king whose throne has been usurped but who bore no grudge, assuming a needless guilt instead.

"Good morning, miss. It is my hope that I did not disturb you." The faded blue eyes looked straight into hers. A little breeze moved the white goatee from right to left, then back again. Kitty smiled in recognition. She had known even before she heard the crisp, clean English accent the identity of her caller.

"You are not disturbing me in the least," she said, opening the door wide enough to accommodate the roundness of him. "I am delighted to see you, Colonel!"

Colonel Witham entered, his shoulders properly erect, his expression unchanged. "I've come to say goodbye, miss, and I prefer to stand, thank you," he said when Kitty motioned toward the barrel-back chair nearest him.

"I don't understand," she said slowly. "I understood that you—well, lived here—and I was looking forward to saying hello, not goodbye."

For a flickering second she thought there was surprise in the pale eyes. If so, he wiped it away with firm discipline.

"I am acting according to your wishes, miss."

"Colonel Witham, I've no idea what you're talking about. It is most certainly not my wish that you should leave here. As a matter of fact, until I can get some loose ends of business tied up, I am not in a position to assume full responsibility here. Won't you sit down and let's talk—*please*."

"As you wish, miss."

The man was so genuine, so forthright, that Kitty knew he would appreciate the same quality

in others. "Tell me what caused you to feel
unwelcome here," she said, seating herself on a lop-
sided hassock.

By way of reply Colonel Witham handed a busi-
ness-size envelope to Kitty. The return address
confirmed the suspicion which had been growing
since the Colonel's greeting. GOTSCHALK & GOT-
SCHALK, it read. And the terse message ordered
the Colonel to "vacate said premises on or before
June 10."

Kitty stared at the letter in disbelief. "They had
no right without consulting me. It's true that I
am not the legal owner of the ranch. But I will
be!"

"Either way, miss, I was led to believe that my
presence here was a nuisance. It makes little difference whether you or they are proprietors."

"*They?* Who, Colonel?"

Stroking his pointed white beard and finding it
smooth, the Colonel said, "Your lawyers, miss. Is it
not they who hold the mortgage?"

"Mr. Gotschalk—Rhett—why, that's *preposterous—*"

The sinking hassock would no longer support
Kitty's weight. It seemed to be sinking to the floor,
taking her with it. Quickly she stood up. "I'll make
us some tea—I think there's ice—"

"No ice—just a spot of tea."

No ice. The world was falling apart for them both,
and she had insulted her father's English friend by
trying to ice his tea! The laugh she gave in the
kitchen was one of near-hysteria. *Put the kettle
on...concentrate on little things like no ice...* and
HAVE NO FEAR!

Kitty's composure returned. A little shaken but

controlled, she set the tea things on the low table between her and Colonel Witham a few minutes later. To her surprise, the man immediately stood, poured a cup of tea, and handed it to her before pouring another for himself.

"I am a gentleman's gentleman," he said. "I say, do you have a twist of lemon?"

"Then why are you serving ladies?" Kitty teased as she took a lemon from the table centerpiece and sliced it.

"Thank you, miss." The Colonel wrung juice into the steaming tea and took an exploratory sip before picking up the conversation. "I serve where I am needed but prefer being a personal attendant rather than a *valet de chambres*. I do my job extraordinarily well, if I may say so," he said with pride. It was almost as if he were asking for employment.

"I'm sure you do," she said, meaning it. "How did you come to know my father?"

"Master Larry was but a lad when I served your paternal grandfather back on the Continent. But the *blitz*—ah, that changed the entire world. I served Her Majesty's crown, and after the war I came to the Colonies . . ." His voice wavered slightly, then staunchly he added, "where I remained as confidant to your father."

The statement prompted a million questions in Kitty's mind. It also brought an awareness of how important it was for this man to remain at the "Circle Left"—important for both of them. She said as much and promised to take care of the matter with the attorneys. When she saw the rim of tears in the Colonel's eyes, she shifted the subject back to her father. It would be an indignity, she was sure, for a gentleman's gentleman to weep.

"So my father was English. Tell me all about him, as much as your time will allow," she begged.

"It is your time which is at premium, miss. I suggest that we follow your schedule."

Kitty suggested that they could work and talk—if he knew how to hang kitchen curtains? Indeed, he did! And the look in his face was one of gratitude. His eyes reminded her of Jane Doe's—reflecting the need to be needed.

Colonel Witham was unable to answer all her questions because there had been a time lapse between his having seen Master Larry, the small boy, and Lawrence Fairfield, the man. Kitty's grandfather, once he had established himself in the "New World," wrote for his friend to join him. By the time Colonel Witham (his Christian name was Conrad, he told her) had put his affairs in order in London and come to America, her grandfather was no longer alive. But she *was* aware of his business with the film producers?

Kitty, her mouth filled with curtain hooks, shook her head. At the gesture, the Colonel's manner became more guarded. "I supposed your attorneys had told you—here, miss, hand me the hooks. You could bloody well swallow one, you know."

Kitty obliged with a smile. "Was there more than one company involved?"

He secured a hook before answering. "There were three, miss," he said in a positive voice.

"*Three?* Three companies used the 'Circle Left' as a setting? What kind of films? Wouldn't that bring in a great deal of money?"

"A sizable amount. And in addition your father

kept the horses for filming the Westerns. Unfortunately, he did not manage his money well, if I may say so—"

"But you're saying there should be income yet?"

"The contracts are still in effect, it is true."

Impulsively Kitty reached out a hand and tugged at the sleeve of his sweater. "Never mind the curtains—we're almost finished—but what you're saying is more important. How do you know these things, Colonel? How can you be sure?"

"Why, I supposed the law firm had informed you that it was Mr. Fairfield's wish that I keep a duplicate set of books. He could be very thorough. Everything he did was done with a certain style. Take this house: It is built to last—will you release my arm now in order that I may finish my task?"

Kitty withdrew her hand absentmindedly. Her father managed all things well except money—and love. Knowing that, he had made sure that somewhere there would be a record of his finances. When the Colonel asked for "one final hook," she placed it in his hand and let her mind drift back to its wandering. "Circle Left" was income property. Rhett had not told her. Mr. Gotschalk had been vague. And Clayton had clammed up. Thank goodness, there was a record in this dependable man's possession. With that thought came a sudden revelation.

"Why weren't the taxes paid?" she blurted out.

The Colonel climbed down from the chair on which he had climbed to adjust the gathering of a top ruffle. "They were," he said simply. "I will bring you the receipt and go over the books with you tomorrow—no tomorrow is the Sabbath. Will Monday fit in with your schedule?" Kitty nodded.

"I am very confused—but grateful. You are a darling!" On sudden impulse, she leaned forward and kissed the smooth, round cheek.

"Thank you, miss. It has been a pleasant afternoon. Consider me in your debt and know that my services are available. We should get at the rock garden, shouldn't we now?"

"There's so much I need to ask," Kitty said as the Colonel turned as if to leave. "The rock garden— yes. We can work as we talk. I have questions about my parents. And there are some things you can fill me in on about Rhett Dawson and Clayton Madrone."

At the door, Colonel Witham paused, as if debating whether to pursue one of the three subjects and, if so, which one. When he spoke, the names he mentioned were in reverse order. "Clayton Madrone, ah yes, there's a commendable young chap. As was his father before him, but his mother— suffice it to say that she cast a long shadow. Mr. Dawson," Kitty was sure his erect body stiffened, "I do not know very well."

Kitty hoped he would go on to sketch the man as he saw him, better preparing her for meeting Rhett again. Instead, he went back to the subject of her parents. "I knew very little of your mother, except that she was fair of face and that your father mourned the loss of her as one mourns the death of a mate. I really must not keep you—"

"Why did she leave, Colonel? *Why?* All my life I had been led to believe that another woman came between them—"

"Precisely. The first wife."

"She came back—" Kitty's voice faltered and she had difficulty breathing.

"Yes, miss. In a sense, that is correct. The past that one does not understand is a bitter rival, as demonstrated in both the Fairfield and Madrone families ...forgive me, I am out of order. This is all very awkward. I rarely talk so much."

"You have nothing to apologize for," Kitty assured him. "You have helped me so much. If I understand right, the rival my mother feared was out of my father's life? But she wrestled with a shadow? What happened to the other woman?"

The Colonel sighed. "Ah, who knows? That was of little consequence. The second Mrs. Fairfield could never accept that her husband loved her. Jealousy is the sister of love, perhaps, but it well may be the brother of the devil as well! ' 'Tis a monster begot upon itself, born on itself...the green-eyed monster which doth mock the meat it feeds on.' "

"Shakespeare," Kitty responded idly, her mind still on her mother, who had confused jealousy with love, perpetuating suspicions and fears until they became truths to her.

"...Shakespeare, yes," the Colonel was saying. " 'Trifles light as air are to the jealous confirmations...' Will there be anything else, miss?"

Her guest, who belonged here, was waiting to be dismissed. Never! "Yes, there is something else, sir." Kitty waited, in hopes that her use of the title would communicate a reversal of roles. But the Colonel remained silent, his face immobile. "Promise that you will remain."

"As you wish, miss, but—" His voice was cut

short by the ringing of the phone. Kitty hurried to answer. "Rhett?" she said, surprised. "One moment—" but when she turned the Colonel was gone.

11

Rhett stood in the middle of the living room, hands on hips as if ready to draw, legs slightly akimbo, giving the impression that otherwise his head would bump the ceiling. Casually he glanced about him, approval in his eyes, but he said nothing.

"Sit down," Kitty invited. "Every muscle I have is aching. When you called, I was hanging curtains."

"You shouldn't be doing work like that alone, Kit. In fact—" He paused, easing himself into the chair she offered.

"I should not be living here alone," Kitty finished

for him. "I know your feeling about that. But this is what I want, Rhett—where I want to be. It is home. I felt it from the beginning, and I feel it all the more after what Colonel Witham has told me."

"The Colonel! Has that old codger been pestering you?" The words might have been fired from a gun.

"Pestering me? Not at all." Kitty was about to demand why the eviction notice had gone to her father's friend without her approval, then decided against it. Why not let one of the partners—the one who handled business affairs of the "Circle Left," according to Mr. Gotschalk—have an opportunity to explain? So, instead of asking, she said, "I find him helpful and informative."

"Listen, Kit," Rhett leaned forward, his tone almost pleading, "you must know that I have your best interests at heart. I cautioned you to be careful. . .I have myself to blame for not getting here sooner—looking after you and keeping him away. He lives in the past, imagines the rest."

Rhett's voice was filled with self-criticism—that of a little boy admitting his wrongdoings, asking for forgiveness while begging for no punishment. It said that there was no real irregularity here, that everything could be straightened out—which was probably true. Kitty's laugh was as much at herself as at the man who was here to help her.

"You have no need to blame yourself. Nothing happened, Rhett. I'm just glad you're here. Now, tell me all that has happened."

Rhett's face lit up. "This, this—and *this*!" With an air of triumph, he laid a stack of official-looking envelopes before her, fanning them out for her to see.

"My identifications! Oh, they've come. And sooner than I expected. . . I own the property? It's mine?"

Rhett grinned boyishly and Kitty felt her doubts begin to dissolve. There was still a lot that needed explaining, a lot she would need to ask about, seek advice on. . .but what was he saying?

". . .and so, if you would like to have me meet the back taxes, I will. Just consider it a loan."

"But, Rhett—" Kitty hesitated, uncertain how to phrase the question without mentioning her source of information. She swallowed and began again, "Are you sure they aren't paid up? Couldn't there be a mistake?"

Rhett took the hand she had injured between his palms. Feeling the Band-Aid, he said sympathetically, "Hey, now! What have we here?"

"It's nothing—nothing at all," Kitty assured him, then went on to tell him about the accident, Clayton's coming, and their trip to town. It was easy to see that Rhett was displeased.

"Why didn't you call *me*, little one? I told you—"

"I know what you told me, Rhett," she said a little impatiently. Rhett deserved better. She softened her voice. "It wouldn't have mattered. You were away— probably on your way to the 'Circle Left,' according to Mr. Gotschalk. *Were* you here the day before yesterday? Somebody was. The door was open and the dog was out—"

Rhett stared at her in disbelief. Gripping her hand so hard that it hurt, a deep blush stained his neck and rushed up the full length of his face to stain the white rim at his hairline. "Are you saying. . .I would go snooping around. . .

Kit, could you really think that of me?"

Of course she couldn't. Kitty apologized. Rhett kissed the palm of her hand gently and curled her fingers into a fist. "Keep it," he said lightly. The awkward moment between them was gone. He picked up the conversation.

Rhett had been here, yes. He checked the fences to make sure they were all in good repair. They were. But (he frowned) did she know that some of the horses seemed to have strayed onto the "Circle Right"? No—but she would check with Clayton. Better not (Rhett smiled tolerantly). It would be better if he himself were the target of Clayton's rage if he were in one of his moods. "We call him 'Madrone, the Mad Minister,' " Rhett grinned, picking up his hat and tracing the circumference with a deeply tanned finger.

Kitty felt the urge to say something in Clayton's defense but let the matter go in favor of getting back to the topic from which they had strayed. "The taxes—Rhett—I can't let you pay . . . oh, the mortgage! Do you—?"

Before she could finish the question as to who held the mortgage, Rhett broke in with a laugh. "Hey, hey! One dragon at a time! Supposing I made the loan big enough to cover both the taxes and the mortgage? You can repay me when you dispose of the property."

"*Dispose* of it?" Kitty cried out in dismay. "Didn't Mr. Gotschalk tell you that the 'Circle Left' isn't for sale?"

"Kit honey, you can't mean you really plan to *stay!*" Rhett sounded genuinely alarmed. His eyebrows arched so high they almost touched the shock of brown hair that fell over his forehead.

Kitty laughed. "One doesn't come to Arizona for the summer."

"But I told you it wasn't safe. There have been some strange things going on around here...and the place is in the red."

Rhett was obviously distraught, genuinely concerned about her. Kitty decided against telling him about the frightening incidents since her arrival. It would cause him more concern. Instead, she reminded him that he had offered to make her a loan and that she would think about that. But her staying on would take no further consideration. Her mind was made up.

"Whatever you want, of course, little darlin'." Apparently Rhett had relaxed, for his Western drawl had returned.

"One would think you're trying to get rid of me," she teased. Seeing the red flush return, Kitty knew she had embarrassed him again. Before she could apologize Rhett had risen to his full height and seemed to be examining his boots. He stooped to flick dust from one toe. When he stood up, his embarrassment had vanished.

"You know better than that!" Without warning he took a giant step toward her, reached out his long arms, and drew her to him. "The opposite's true," Rhett said against her hair, his voice ringing with sincerity. "What I want is to *keep* you. It's too soon to ask this, but I'm going to ask it anyway, trying to keep ahead of the stampede of other eligible men. We belong together, Kit. One day you'll realize that—"

"Rhett—" There was much to talk about, and he was leading her astray. This was too soon...too soon...confusing!

"Now, now, just stay put here where you're safe in my arms. I've fallen in love with you, little Kit-Cat...tell me, do you believe in love at first sight?"

Kitty closed her eyes to the problems confronting her. Did she believe in love at first sight? Well, yes, she did. It had happened to her. But it was not Rhett with whom she had fallen in love. It was Clay—who, ironically, did not want to be loved. Clay was the most intelligent, the most attractive, the most irresistible man she had ever met...and yet it was the man in whose arms she stood who made *her* feel irresistible! "It's not fair—it's not fair—" Kitty cried out, pulling herself away.

"What is it, little one? What did I do—or say?"

"Go—please go, Rhett. It's something I can't explain—"

"There *is* something between you and Madrone then?" His words came slowly, as if he believed the worst. But at the moment Kitty could not bring herself to deny the implied accusation that there was more than met the eye to her being in Clay's house. "Don't let it happen, Kit—not again. He's not what he seems. He'll make overtures of love, try to convert you like the Indians, then break your heart like he broke Colette's. I can't stand by and let that happen again. He'll go to any means—"

"Stop, Rhett. Please don't say any more. He has done nothing. Please, you *have* to go." Her voice dropped to a whisper. When he did not move, a sudden forcefulness rose within her—a strength she did not know she possessed. "Get out!"

Moments later she heard his car start, then—with a spray of gravel—roar down the road leading away from the "Circle Left." Only then did she fall trembling onto the couch, where she lay sobbing for all she had found out . . . and then what she had not found out. The conversation had gone wrong— all wrong. The questions she had for Rhett hung over her unanswered—because she had let things get out of hand? Or was it that this man who claimed to see every person he met as a potential friend was not what he appeared to be—making her afraid to confide in him?

"Which of these people can I trust?" The words came as a little prayer. "And which ones should I fear, Lord?"

Almost as if by answer, Jane Doe dragged her bloated body to the couch, whined, and licked out a long, wet tongue to dry her tears. "You, of course! I can trust *you*. And we can trust our Maker . . . how about the one who led us to Him, pal?"

Jane Doe stretched out her pink tongue again. This time Kitty was prepared. She ducked, laughed, and stood up. Her heart felt lighter. If there was an enemy, the Lord would reveal him.

Clayton came to pick her up earlier than Kitty expected him. "I'm sorry. I forgot to ask what time," she called as Jane Doe waddled out to meet him. "I just have to swish my hair up and—"

"What's wrong with it the way it is? I like it. We can drive with the top of the car down." He patted Jane Doe and began coaxing her into the house. "Lock her in."

Kitty nodded and put on her sunglasses. She must look like a witch, with her hair drooping around the wide straps of the cotton dress, which there had been no time to change. But she felt a sense of excitement as they rode beneath the ripe Arizona sun. It was good to have broken the habit of a lifetime...to let her hair blow free ...and, temporarily, to let her problems blow along with it. Unconsciously she smiled and, seeking Clayton's face, saw that he smiled in return. The noise of the wind made conversation impossible. The silence was companionable, adding to the Sunday feel of the bright, blue morning.

Once Clayton had seated Kitty inside the church, he excused himself to speak with the minister in his study, promising to be back shortly. At first she felt uncomfortable, wondering if a multitude of curious eyes were focused on her. When at last she dared look up, nobody seemed to have noticed. Well, that was comforting—as was the fact that other women in the small congregation were dressed as casually for the heat as she.

To Kitty's surprise, she recognized some of the people. Shopkeepers who had helped her. The Colonel. She wondered briefly why Clayton had not asked him to ride along with them. Then she caught sight of Mr. Gotschalk in a pew farther toward the back, seemingly engaged in conversation with a much younger man. Could that be his son? Rhett was not there. Kitty realized with a shock that she had not expected to see him.

"He'll try to convert you like the Indians... go to any means...." Puzzling over her problems and Rhett's strange behavior, she had let his remarks about Clayton pass. Now, like a mild taste with a powerful aftertang, they came back.

Then Clayton was slipping into the seat beside

her and they were sharing a hymnal as the first strains of organ music commenced. Again she had the feeling that the two of them could be a happily married couple, worshiping together. Her hand brushed his beneath the hymnal and she jerked it away with such a sudden motion that the book went closed. She dared not look at him. Her love would reveal itself—maybe even ask for an answer he was not ready to give. With all her heart, she wished the situation were reversed. *Please, Lord, let it happen someday*, she pleaded silently, and then concentrated on the simple and direct sermon the elderly minister delivered.

People gathered around her after the service, giving her a sense of belonging. Yes, Kitty told them, she would be remaining here...and, yes, she would be attending church...this was home.

Yet through it all she had a sense of detachment—a feeling of *otherwhereness*, if there was such a word. She was an actress from whom the production people were keeping the story line all mystery and intrigue. She was saying lines that were not quite clear to her at the time. But it was a pleasant feeling. God, who knew the end from the beginning, had taken over completely here in this little church. The answers would come when she needed them...and suddenly she and Clayton were waving goodbye...on their way home to the Sunday roast...a quiet afternoon in which she would wash her hair while he worked on his tapes...then an evening under the stars....

It came as no surprise when he said suddenly, "Would you like to come home with me?"

"Of course," she said without hesitation. Then, as he started the engine, she realized how forward she had been. Should she say something? "I guess you'll want to show me the material I'm to type?" Silence. She would try again—lightly. "If you're convinced that I'm not a reporter here to get your story?"

"I thought we settled that."

"We did—and I didn't mean to keep bringing up the past—" Kitty realized that her words were all wrong. Clayton was sure to read something into them she did not intend. She stole a look at his face. He was regarding her with that intent look that made her uncomfortable. But she was a new person in more ways than one. And so, instead of putting the matter aside, as she once would have, Kitty said, "I do want you to know that I have all my identification now. The ranch should soon be mine."

Clayton's change of mood was swift. "Congratulations!" he said with a smile. "You mean it's all clear?"

They had sat with the engine running, oblivious to the heat of the noonday sun. *That's how it is when we talk*, Kitty thought. *We shut the whole world out.*

She realized then that Clayton was putting the top of the convertible up. ". . . so we can talk," he said.

Kitty told him about the Colonel's visit as the car hummed along the blacktop road. Yes, he knew about the second set of books. . .and, no, he did *not* know about the eviction notice! "And Rhett didn't seem to either," she said. "He'd have told me—"

"You realize, of course, that one of them, Dawson or Gotschalk, is lying!"

The sharpness of his voice and use of such strong language surprised her. "Clay, do you know more than you're telling?"

"Do *you*?"

"Maybe I do," Kitty said slowly as Clayton wheeled into his driveway and eased to a stop. Haltingly, then, she told him about Rhett's visit, omitting only the advances he had made. "Why would he lie to me, Clay?" she asked instead. "Or withhold information?"

Clayton opened the door and reached out his hand to Kitty. "Has he told you he wants to purchase the land?"

Kitty's heart skipped a beat and then seemed to stop altogether. She shook her head dazedly and took his hand, feeling the world around her begin to go into slow motion. Unable to find her voice, she raised wide, questioning eyes to Clayton.

"Oh, Kitten!" His hands supported her gently and the tone of voice was self-deprecating. "How clumsy of me. I'm sorry." He seemed about to say more, but a woman's friendly voice was calling from behind the front screen door.

"Come in out of this heat, you two!"

Then, without seeming to move at all, they were inside the homey living room of the "Circle Right." Mrs. Donohue, a thin, wrinkled, ageless woman, introduced herself as the housekeeper and sometimes-cook.

"Oh, not that Clayton here works his maid-servants on the Sabbath, mind you! But I feel the Lord reckons I should feed the body while Clayton and the Reverend feed the souls. Wouldn't you say, Miss Fairfield?"

Promising dinner in ten minutes, Mrs. Donohue was off to the kitchen again. Clayton was by Kitty's side immediately. "Forgive me—and let's not allow my thoughtless words to ruin our day. You'll want to wash up."

Kitty looked briefly at him. She could not fathom what she saw in his expression. It was something like anger. Not at her. At Rhett, she was sure. But his face said more: "Discussion closed." She turned and hurried down the hall.

In the familiar coolness of the bathroom, Kitty washed her burning face. This was only her second visit here, and yet Clayton's house felt like home- just as she had known its owner two weeks and had come to think of him as her property, like the "Circle Left." She owned neither of them yet, but she would!

The thought came so surprisingly that Kitty realized she was rubbing her face too vigorously with the rough green towel. Turning to replace it, she saw the same assortment of lovely dressing gowns. Hadn't Colette said she had come for her things? She left the bathroom banging the door behind her.

"Wow!" Clayton's voice from down the hall sounded amused. "Somebody's in for trouble."

"I thought she was clearing out." Kitty had not known she was going to speak the words.

Clayton looked at her blankly. And then slowly his face cleared.

"Oh, the dressing gowns? If you must know, Miss Nosy, they belong to my sister. Jana made them for herself. Now, is there anything more you would like to know?"

Shame flooded over Kitty. She had made a spectacle of herself. To cover her embarrassment, she shrugged. "I am not a reporter," she said coldly.

13

The Sunday roast that Mrs. Donohue set before Clayton, as envisioned in Kitty's domestic fantasy, became a reality. The rest of the fantasy did not. The telephone rang as Clayton began the carving.

"I'll get it." Mrs. Donohue rose from the table but in moments was back. "The fences are down—horses out—Mr. Dawson says there's real trouble—you and Miss Fairfield should know, he says—" The words came out breathlessly.

Clayton sprang to his feet. His face was darker than the clouds which were beginning to pile themselves into threatening shapes along the horizon. Something spelled danger. Kitty jumped to her feet and followed Clayton down the hall toward the front door.

"You go back. Stay here until I'm finished." The words were an order. Kitty ignored it and grabbed at his sleeve.

"I'm going with you, Clay! The call was for me, too—"

Clayton whirled to face her. "That's the whole point. It could be a trick. Bait for you—no, you don't see at all. Let go of my arm. There's danger!"

"All the more reason I want to be with you—" But he was gone. Moments later the pickup she had seen parked on the west ell of the ranch house roared east toward the back of the property, where, Rhett had told her, there was a "secret road." Rhett! He had mentioned the fences and that her horses strayed.

Helplessly, Kitty turned back to the table, where the food was getting cold. Her appetite was gone, but the gnawing in her stomach was more from fear than hunger. Mrs. Donohue was picking up the dishes and chatting away like a magpie. Only half-hearing what the woman said, Kitty began to help. It was better to keep busy. *Please, Lord,* her heart was saying.

". . . so don't you be worrying about Clayton. He's a God-fearing, God-loving man, but he can be mighty tough when the situation demands. This desert's no place for softies. That's why he worries about you—not that the *word* applies, mind you. But he thinks you oughtn't be alone. Says he's got his reasons." Mrs. Donohue picked up the gravy boat.

"Do you know what they are, Mrs. Donohue?" Kitty asked without meeting the older woman's eye.

"Not for sure. Something to do with somebody's spooking the place, you know? Trying to scare you like they did in 'Gas Light'?" Mrs. Donohue turned toward the kitchen with Kitty close at her heels. She was listening now, hanging onto every word. "He wanted to bring you here, just to make sure you'd be safe until the deed was in your hands—maybe longer, who's to say?" Kitty felt herself blush at Mrs. Donohue's smile.

"But he couldn't bring himself to trust me—or any other woman, could he?" Kitty asked, setting a stack of unused china on the counter.

"He's going to trust you with his typing. That's something!" Mrs. Donohue said, rolling up her sleeves and testing the tapwater before adding detergent. "If you want to dry, we'll do these kettles right. Never put much trust in that dishwasher Clayton's father bought for Mrs. Madrone. Never was satisfied, that woman. She wasn't the maternal type, believe me. It would have been a blessing if she'd been barren—never should've married, if you ask me. That woman's responsible for the beginnings of pain for Clayton, bless his heart. And then that movie star up and did him in."

Mrs. Donohue plunged her hands into the billowing suds and smiled in satisfaction. Kitty picked up a snowy dishtowel. "What happened to Clay's mother?" she prompted.

"An embarrassment to Mr. Madrone, his only problem being he wore a blind bridle where she was concerned, refused to believe any of the stories.

She was a beauty, you know...wasn't exactly a movie star, just an *entertainer*, you know?" At Kitty's puzzled frown, she added in a subdued whisper, "Lots of 'uncles,' she kept bringing around to introduce to those innocent children. Then, one day, she up and disappeared, leaving a note that she was filing for divorce. The children were on their own, but you don't fool kids—they'd known. But not her husband—it killed him. And in a sense it killed Clayton, too. Something inside of him died."

Kitty nodded, fascinated and horrified. Before her flashed a picture of the self-contained Clayton Madrone as he must have been as a confused, frightened child. That was why, she was sure now, he avoided discussions about his childhood and why he feared involvement with women, too. She could see him as a vulnerable, hurt, and lonely boy. That revealed to her another face. And for a fleeting second, she felt a strong maternal urge to hold and comfort him. The idea died quickly.

"What about Colette?" Inwardly scolding herself for questioning the talkative housekeeper, Kitty felt driven to know the truth.

Mrs. Donohue wiped her hands on her apron and went on talking without hesitation. "A regular Jezebel, that one! Clayton had shied away from women until she blew in like the dust-devil she was! Worked her way in here claiming to be too delicate to live in the trailers provided by the film producers...and (Mrs. Donohue's voice took on a falsetto intended to sound like that of the actress) *if she could just have a bite of this—oh, darling, you wouldn't believe the food!* Well, before Clayton could say 'Jack Robinson' she'd talked him into letting her

occupy a room. . .*those awful beds, darling!* You'd
have to see her to understand how he could have
swallowed that."

Full lips curved in laughter. . .eyes filled with
promise. . .all for Clayton. "I've seen her," Kitty said,
feeling her heart ache with something akin to envy.
"What did she do to him?"

"She stole his heart—and then she stole the plot
to a novel he was writing. The whole thing was a
put-up job between her and the film company.
Clayton could have sued but refused—just ended
things between them—and she turned to Rhett."

"*Rhett!*" Kitty almost dropped the plate she was
drying. "You mean—"

"I mean they're married—off and on. Talk has it
that he makes a lot of money from some shady deals
with the law firm, enough that Colette hangs on—
going her way, like they do in this new generation.
Clayton grew a beard, hid out like Jonah—"

There was a loud clap of thunder which drowned
out the rest of Mrs. Donohue's words. Kitty had
lost track of time, but now she was keenly aware
that Clayton had been gone too long. . .that he
could be in danger from the lightning, which
seemed to be striking close by, and from the situation regarding the livestock . . .and then there was
Jane Doe. . .

"I have to get home. The dog's shut up alone. She's
afraid of storms and she'll get alarmed—do you have
a car?"

The woman shook her head. Clayton drove "across
the wash" to get her, she said. Besides, she was
supposed to show Miss Fairfield the recording
room (did she know he prepared the minister's
sermons, too?). . .and there was the typewriter

. . .and her assignments. Mrs. Donohue became very agitated, but Kitty was adamant. "I have to go. Do you have the keys to Clayton's convertible? We'll exchange cars tomorrow."

Reluctantly Mrs. Donohue handed her the keys. And Kitty braced herself against the storm.

14

Rain coursed down the windshield faster than the wipers could sweep it away, making vision impossible. The only recourse was to leave the window down, Kitty decided, and try to see ahead from the side. Wind whipped the rain inside the car, soaking the upholstery and winding her wet hair blindingly about her face, mingling with her tears.

Her headlight beams picked up the scene ahead. Dips in the road where mirages had shimmered promisingly such a short while ago were now roaring rivers. Well, God had divided the Red

Sea for Moses. He would do no less for her in this private exodus. *Make me strong in my time of weakness, Lord!* Gripping the wheel, she desperately drove on.

A blue-white flash of lightning showed the cook shack where the Colonel lived. In confusion she pulled into the lake that had served as a driveway in dry weather and leaned on the horn. The Colonel's door did not open. And there was no light in the window. He, too, was gone.

As Kitty stared out the windshield, wondering if she should try to drive on, a tattoo of hailstones exploded against it, cracking it like a zigzag of lightning. At the same moment a violent gust of wind struck the car with such force that Kitty was sure it would overturn. There was no choice; she must go on.

Kitty had no clear memory of getting home. She remembered that the earth seemed to shake and tremble around her. Then there came the feeling that there was no ground at all—just water. She was Noah . . . floating in an ark . . . going to pick up the animal which would replenish the earth. . . .

And suddenly she was safe in her house. *Safe?* She didn't know. It was enough to be home—to be welcomed by frenzied whines and warm canine kisses. Impulsively she threw her arms around Jane Doe and whispered, "He'll make it, Janie, he'll make it to the ark in time . . . ."

When she let herself give in to a torrent of tears, Jane Doe joined her with a low, lonely cry of understanding. Then its tone changed to a wail that sounded like a sob. Instinctively Kitty knew that the sound was born of pain. *The puppies!*

"Oh, Janie, *Janie!*" she said in bewilderment. "I don't think this is the way the story goes—are you sure there were puppies born in the ark?"

A bed. The dog would need a bed. Forgetting that she was soaked to the skin, Kitty rushed into the spare bedroom in search of a box. The room was in darkness. She fumbled for the light switch, found it, and pushed it upward. The light she had expected did not come. No electricity!

Hurrying back to the kitchen, Kitty located a candle and lighted it. The candlelight cast a ghostly glow over the old trunks, which were layered in dust and strung together with cobwebs. Here was her past . . . a past which had lain undisturbed since father packed these possessions away at the time of her mother's departure. But out there lay her future . . . the world of the living . . . something which needed her.

And with the calm which was becoming a part of her now, Kitty dumped the contents of the largest box she could handle—pausing only long enough to pick up what looked like a tiny jewelry box—and hurried back to the living room. Jane Doe was pacing the floor and letting out low moans.

"Steady, pal, steady." Over and over Kitty repeated the words reassuringly as she laid the jewel box on the dining room table beneath the swinging fern, cut away the front side of the cardboard carton, and padded it with an old Army blanket.

"This is the delivery room!" Kitty said softly as she placed the box before Jane Doe. The dog took her word for it and got inside—which was comforting. "Neither of us knows much about 'woman's travail,' but we'll find out together."

The rain had turned into a steady downpour, but Kitty was unaware of the heavy drumming on the roof. With single-mindedness she squatted beside the box and stroked the dog's convulsing sides.

Hours seemed to pass. Her body ached from her cramped position, but she dared not leave. Each time she made an attempt to shift her weight slightly, Jane Doe's great, brown eyes widened with fear. When they closed, Kitty aroused her. "I think you're supposed to stay awake and push down."

Oh, dear God, I don't think either of us can go on much longer! Kitty's anguished prayer went up just as the front door swung open. Clayton! Clayton, pulling her to her feet. Telling her she looked like a drowned rat. Clayton, holding her close—not caring how she looked...

And then pushing her aside! "Hit the shower, you! On the double. You may be needed. Okay, Jane Doe, on your feet like a good girl! The Colonel helped with horses, but this is woman's work!"

He love me, he loves me not, the hiss of the shower mocked. But too much had happened this strange day for Kitty to put it all together. She must play out this scenario like a computerized robot...towel dry...get into dry clothing...and hurry back. Jane Doe needed her. And Clayton needed her too! With that thought her head cleared and she hurried back into the living room, where the miracle of birth was taking place.

Again she lost track of time. Dimly she was aware of handing Clayton what he asked for.

Scissors. Clean rags. Mineral oil. And then there were five beautiful brown-and-white puppies bedded down beside a proud mother. "You get to bed, my Kitten-Eyed one!" Clayton was saying, scooping her in his arms and carrying her into the bedroom, where he placed her on the bed and pulled a light blanket over her. But she fought sleep.

Inside there was a feeling of deep elation. Why then did her eyelids droop? And her mind play tricks on her? Surely, she thought from behind closed lids, Clayton wasn't kissing her in such a soft and gentle manner. What face was this? But her heavy lids would not respond to the question.

"Sleep well. I'll be right in the next room on the couch—watching over Jane Doe," Clayton said softly.

"Lucky dog—" Kitty mumbled. But she was too far into the antechamber of sleep to hear him chuckle.

• • •

It was scarcely light when the Colonel knocked on her door the next morning. For a second Kitty wondered why he was there, all memory wiped out by sleep. "The rock garden, miss. I've come to help."

After all that she had been through, the announcement seemed anticlimactical. Kitty, managing a straight face, invited him in. "Excuse the looks of the house," she murmured. "We went through a lot yesterday, and last night Clayton stayed—"

She stopped, feeling a hot, red flush begin at the tip of her toes and flood her entire body. "I mean— he—I—"

Helplessly bogged down in an explanation that sounded false even to her own ears, Kitty glanced at her guest from the corner of her eye. His expression had not changed.

"Yes, miss, I understand," he said, not saying what it was he understood. "We changed automobiles while you took a few winks. I'll make tea for us—I say, have you some English muffins or scones?"

Wordlessly Kitty allowed him to take over, pointing to the breadbox as she reached for the little jewel case she had found last night. Curiously she lifted the lid and then gave a gasp of pleasure. Inside lay a pair of tiny cameo earrings, and about them wound a ribboned cameo necklace.

"Colonel Witham!" Kitty held her treasure for him to see.

The man nodded and went on measuring tea into a teaball. "I am glad you kept this culinary piece. Teabags offer less aroma than plastic roses . . . ah, yes, I remember the cameo set. Your father's gift to the woman he loved—if ever she returned. They've never been worn, you know. But the books will tell you all about their tragic love. I've brought them for your examination. After a spot of tea."

Kitty accepted the cup that Colonel Witham handed her and was about to set it down when she saw a small piece of paper, folded to fit beneath the jewelry box. In her excitement she had overlooked it. Even before unfolding it, she knew the note was left there by Clayton.

> *Hi! I've gone to the village to apply for a license for you as a K-9 midwife! You were Miss Wonderful last night. By the way, the fences are mended between us—the ones that hold horses in, that is. Think we can patch up the others? The Colonel will look after you until we can talk. C.*

Kitty held the note to her heart, aware suddenly of hunger. She wanted to sing, shout, and dance the Colonel around the room! Instead, she ate the plate of poached eggs he set before her and asked for a second muffin. "*Now*," she said meekly in what she hoped was a good-girl voice, "may I make myself some coffee?"

"I shall attend to the coffee, miss, while you attend to the newborns."

Kitty picked up the wriggling puppies one-by-one under Jane Doe's watchful eye. Then, promising the new mother that her babies were in good hands, she opened the back door and said, "Don't you want a stroll?"

The dog paused on the threshold to sniff suspiciously. Then, bristles up, she gave a low, throaty growl. It was natural that she would be more protective, Kitty decided, and almost pushed her through the door. Jane Doe immediately began to sniff beneath the bedroom window. Then, seeming to pick up a trail, she went barking around the house.

"Is the animal vicious, miss?" the Colonel asked in alarm.

"Not usually—it's the puppies, most likely. But

I would think any trail would have been washed away in yesterday's downpour. Unless it's awfully fresh?"

The Colonel promised to investigate later. But for now she was to finish her breakfast. As Kitty drank her coffee, he told her little fragments concerning her parents, adding to the picture she had formed already. One thing puzzled her.

"Did I live here, Colonel Witham?"

"You were born here, miss."

Then she was right in feeling it was home. "But why did he let us go?" The question was torn from her heart.

The Colonel cleared his throat. "Your grandmother came for a visit and your mother agreed with her that it was best for you. Your father was very hurt and said that he would trouble her no more—unless—" Colonel Witham paused. "I suggest that you read the documents for yourself."

"Just finish your sentence—*please*—"

The Colonel picked up her plate. "Will there be anything else, miss?"

Kitty shook her head and waited. As she had hoped, he picked up the conversation. "—unless she returned of her own accord."

Of her own accord. All her mother had to do was assert herself once—just *once*—and say she wished to return. Like the prodigal son, she would have been received in the loving arms of her husband. Then, like the inscription on the urn promised, they would have been together, the three of them, through the years...

Tears filled her eyes for what might have been. Well, it wasn't going to happen to her. Unwittingly, her mother had left her a legacy of wisdom as precious as her father's gift!

"Colonel Witham," she said practically, "where are the books?"

15

"It's all here," Kitty said incredulously to herself hours later. Resolutely she had put aside the packet of letters, although there had been a strong temptation to read them (as she felt her father would have wanted her to). Mostly they bore no postmark and no stamp. Her father's name on the outside of the envelopes which were addressed to her mother said they had never been mailed . . . maybe never finished. But another small packet of envelopes also piqued her curiosity. Tied with a black ribbon and postmarked years before her own birth, they were addressed to her father.

The name on the outside of each was "Gwendolyn Teel." Her father's ledgers were far more important right now. With the mortgage due three days from now...most of the horses missing... questions about ownership...

Well, there could be no question now! The records which the Colonel had kept so faithfully held photostatic copies of her parents' marriage, her birth, the deed, a copy of the will, and—*Praise the Lord!*—a copy of tax payments!

In her exuberance Kitty rushed through the back door and stooped to kiss the round, pink cheek of the Colonel, who was squatting inside what was beginning to resemble the rock garden he promised. Busy with a clump of stubborn-rooted grass, he did not look up. "Thank you, miss."

"Oh, Colonel, it's all here, just as you said—except for one thing. All receipts fail to show how much remains to be paid on the property—"

Colonel Witham pulled up the final grass root. "Bloody persistent, the grasses of the field can be. Ah, yes, the remainder on the principal." He rose to face her. "You are speaking of the loan your father negotiated when he built this house? It was held by the People's Bank in the village."

Was held? "Do you mean—?" Kitty began the question and then stopped. It was impossible that the mortgage could have been met in full. Mr. Gotschalk or Rhett would have known. Could they have held a second mortgage—or—?

"I have to go into the village," she said, spinning on her heel.

Behind her, Kitty heard the Colonel's protests. Miss Kitty wasn't to leave here...orders from the young Mr. Madrone himself! There was danger! His last words were something about tracks. Then his voice died away as she determinedly started the car and headed for the bank in the pueblo.

A thin, young-looking man, seeming eager to impress the bank's customers, answered Kitty's routine questions as to how mortgages, deeds, and titles were handled. "But when it comes down to individual cases, only the computer knows the answers," he said as his fingers busied themselves with countless keys after he had shown her identification to his "superior."

"Strange," the young man said. "Very strange. Are you sure Mr. Fairfield's property—er, your property—is mortgaged? That is, that People's Bank holds a lien? Any foreclosures would show here. We are very thorough. Unless," he hesitated, "it could have been satisfied long ago?"

Kitty explained the situation briefly. When he asked if she had an attorney, she nodded reluctantly. "However," Kitty leaned forward and lowered her voice, "I would prefer we kept this confidential." He was as pleased as she had expected. Oh, of course, they would! People's Bank wanted satisfied customers, and if Miss Fairfield would like to open an account—

"Later," Kitty smiled. "Now, if you would try GOTSCHALK & GOTSCHALK, I will be better prepared when I am settling with them. Then we can discuss an account and other business."

Methodically his fingers flew over the keys again. Then his back stiffened. "Why, yes, I see what has happened. The law firm purchased the mortgage when taxes became delinquent—Miss Fairfield, we haven't finished. *Come back!*"

But Kitty was out of hearing distance. Her feet were beating a tattoo on the walk leading to GOT-SCHALK & GOTSCHALK.

To her surprise, it was Rhett Dawson who opened the door in response to Kitty's knock. "Kit!" The word registered his surprise as well. But he recovered quickly. "Come in, little darlin'—and welcome to my humble abode. Can I get you something cold to drink?"

"No! What you can give me is information. The truth, Rhett. Nothing else will do." Her voice was flat and emotionless. And, for the first time in her life when dealing with a frightening situation, Kitty felt no fear.

"Well, now, of course we want the truth, Kit-Cat. But, first, let's make you cozy—" Rhett advanced toward her.

"Stay away from me!" Kitty spat out the words. "This is not a cozy situation. Why didn't you tell me you three men held the mortgage to the 'Circle Left'?"

Rhett moved back behind his desk, seemingly in charge of the situation. "Oh, I can explain that, darlin'—do sit down now. I'm not going to eat you. In the first place, there really aren't three. My partner thought it looked more impressive to keep the three names when his son pulled out. Good for business, you know. Take small-time businesses like ours—"

"You aren't small-time. I know that!" Kitty cut into his drawl. "And use of the name is about as phony as the other deals you've pulled. Letting me think that some outsider would appear out of nowhere to post a foreclosure sign on my home...letting me think the taxes were delinquent! Now I can no longer believe anything you have said. Why," she paused, suddenly remembering Colette, "you didn't even tell me about your marriage—talked to me about love—"

"Oh, Kit, honey!" One long stride brought Rhett to her side. "I can explain that. Now, you just let old Rhett here tell you what's happened. It's all a mistake—"

Before there was time to escape, she was pinned against his chest. With all her strength, Kitty pushed against him, managing to free her right arm. Praying that her hand would reach the telephone, she thrust it toward the desk. Her reward was the feel of the plastic instrument in her grasp and, before Rhett was aware of what she was doing, she had pushed the button she hoped said "0."

Immediately there was a cool, impersonal voice which filled the room. "Operator!"

With an oath, Rhett released her and grabbed at the telephone. With supernatural strength, Kitty was through the door, down the walk, and inside her car. She had gone as far as she could go. The Lord and His helpers, Clay and his "gentleman's gentleman," must take it from here...

There was so much yet to resolve, but—in spite of the upsetting scene from which she had fled—Kitty felt a strange sort of peace. Her prayer was answered. The enemy was revealed. Clay and Colonel Witham would know how to cope. So thinking, she turned her thoughts to what she had learned today...a better understanding of herself and a better understanding of Clay.

"Well, Lord," she said aloud, "You promised

to make me strong in time of weakness. And You're as good as Your *Word*—no pun intended." Kitty smiled and imagined that her heavenly Father smiled as her own father would have smiled. "I was a lot stronger today than I ever thought I could be, and I'm learning to take myself less seriously. Now, if You and I can just get Clay to take life a little less seriously, too—You will help me, won't You?"

Kitty was almost at the point where the three ranches met in an obtuse angle. She slowed down in preparation for turning up the center road which led to the "Circle Left." Then, on impulse, she made a sharp right turn past the mailbox marked "Promenade Ranch." It seemed important that she know what Rhett's house looked like. It would reveal something of his lifestyle, supported—she felt—by blood money.

The landscape looked the same as that of the neighboring ranches—barren except for sagebrush, rocks, and cacti. But the number of horses surprised her. Hers? Clayton had repaired the fences . . .

And he wanted to mend the fences between herself and him, she remembered with a smile. *I'll know how to deal with him*, she thought. *I understand better, seeing what it's like to be disappointed in love.* Kitty thought of her parents, his parents, his disenchantment with Colette, and her hurt and disappointment in Rhett, who had claimed friendship, then love . . .

When Kitty saw the rambling, red-tiled buildings, she thought for a moment this was the wrong road. Surely this had to be a resort. Everywhere she looked, there were gardens surrounding a Spanish-style stucco castle with a million windows, like on-duty guards, looking in all directions. The gardens surrounded private picnic areas—some sheltered by bright umbrellas; some, by vine-wrapped trellises; and still others, by low, glassed-in walls protecting pools and saunas. The most massive carved door she had ever seen led inside.

Kitty let her eyes wander beyond the house and gardens to the stables in back. There she saw countless riding horses, a training ring, and two enormous Doberman Pinschers on guard. One part of her said this wasn't—it couldn't be—"Promenade Ranch." The other part of her knew that it was.

Sick at heart, she made a U-turn in the circular driveway and drove away faster than was safe. *I don't know what I expected*, she thought. *But it wasn't this. Maybe I hoped for something that would vindicate Rhett...maybe I could not bring myself to believe the truth that God revealed.* Thinking of the shabby office and knowing that it was a deception made her shudder. And for some unexplainable reason she felt driven to get home—*now!*

Kitty had felt no conscious fear, and yet she knew a thrill of relief once she was on the narrow, dusty road leading home. There was so much to tell Clayton—so much to ask him. It occurred to her then that he was supposed to be in the village. Well, they had missed each other. She would tell the Colonel—

But what was he doing in the middle of the road, waving his hands in signal for her to stop? Kitty applied the brakes and stopped, realizing then that they were in front of the cook shack.

"It's been ransacked, miss. My house is in shambles." The Colonel's voice was controlled from force of habit, but there appeared to be a rim of tears around his pale eyes. His face, usually so ruddy, was ashen.

"But what—why? Oh, I'm so sorry!" Kitty climbed from the car and hurried to the man's side. "Are you sure—I mean, could it be a prank—?" But the Colonel was shaking his head. "Vandals?" she asked, casting about for a solution.

"Come see for yourself, miss. Ah, a bit of a shame it is." He pushed open the door and stepped aside.

Kitty glanced about her in disbelief. His desk, all drawers, and the china cupboard had been emptied. The contents were heaped in the middle of the worn carpet. His clothing, jerked from the hooks, was turned inside out and added to the pile, as were the cushions from the divan and chairs. "When did it happen—in broad daylight? And what could they want?"

"Broad daylight, yes, miss. And 'twas the books, I daresay."

The records! Somebody thought they were here. Instead, they were at the "Circle Left." "I must go—" Kitty's words were a whisper. "I must put them in a safe place—"

Again, she heard the Colonel's protests. There had been a call...she was to stay..."gone for several days!" Kitty drove away.

16

It had been a busy, perplexing day. Kitty, trying to put it all behind her until there was time to go over it all and try to make some sense of it, turned the key in the lock of her front door. She was greeted by an overjoyed Jane Doe and the smell of freshly baked food. Hurriedly she checked on the puppies; then, finding them well-cared-for, she followed her nose to the counter beneath the window. "Muffins!" She sniffed appreciatively and was about to bite into one when she saw a note tucked beneath the pan.

"Yorkshire pudding," it read, "is to be eaten

with a fork." Kitty smiled. This one, without an audience, would be eaten as she chose. And then she saw another line in the Colonel's spidery penmanship. "Young Mr. Madrone wishes Miss Kitty to know that business has called him to Los Angeles—"

Los Angeles! Clay had gone to Los Angeles? Whatever took him away must have come up unexpectedly. Kitty felt suddenly engulfed in loneliness and apprehension. *Alone* was a dreadful word. That's why God created Eve for Adam...didn't Clay know?

After a light supper, Kitty lowered and locked the windows, then drew the drapes against the night. She found herself checking the doors repeatedly even though she knew the bolts were secured. The ledgers that Colonel Witham had kept for her father still lay on the combination kitchen-dining-room table because no place she could think of seemed safe. There were the old trunks in the spare bedroom. Maybe one of the barrels—

But the thought of going into the room alone and digging into the once-precious possessions of her father held no appeal. At last, taking the books with her, Kitty went into her bedroom and switched on the bedside light. Remembering that she had forgotten to lay crumpled newspapers beneath the windows and in front of the doors, she went back into the living room. As she worked, Kitty thought she heard Jane Doe growl. Remembering how the dog had sniffed around the windows, she was reminded suddenly that the Colonel had mentioned something about tracks.

I won't think about it. I'm safe. Over and over she reassured herself silently. But there was no escaping the fact that the cook shack had been ransacked—or that Clay was gone.

Finished with the last safety precaution she could think of, Kitty bent down and hugged Jane Doe's neck. "Take care of the babies and me, Janie," she whispered. "You're in charge of security, you know."

At first she lay tense after crawling into bed. Then, when there were no sounds except for the occasional call of a nightbird, she began to relax. Early tomorrow morning she would call the Colonel and they would exchange information.

Picking up the Bible then, Kitty read until her eyes grew heavy. Then, with an unfinished prayer still on her lips, she fell into a deep sleep of sheer exhaustion.

Jane Doe's bark awakened her very early the next morning. But there was nothing alarming about the sound. It was the tail-wagging kind of bark that said a friend was at the door. It was with a wave of relief and affection that she saw the white-bearded Colonel waiting to be admitted.

Over a hearty breakfast which he prepared while she showered, they discussed yesterday's events. The Colonel was no closer to a solution as to who had ransacked his house than before—until Kitty had told him what she had found out at the bank and Rhett Dawson's agitation over her confronting him with the information. Then the pale eyes narrowed slightly in thought. "I say, miss, there has to be a connection here."

Kitty bit her lip in concentration. "It's true that

evidence seems to be piling up," she said slowly. "But when—?"

She stopped then. It would have been possible, yes, for Rhett to take this road when she turned onto the one leading to his ranch. If he was after the books, he would be back. The thought was too awful to face . . . and what would he have done to the Colonel if he had apprehended the intruder? She shuddered.

No! She would not give in to fear. "Colonel," Kitty said, "let's give him the benefit of the doubt until we know. Rhett has done some regrettable things, but I can't think him capable of crime! Now, did Clay tell you when we could expect him home?"

Mr. Madrone would be gone until the end of the week. And, yes, the Colonel knew the nature of his business in the "metropolitan area." He had gone directly to International Films and the two "subsidiary companies," taking along the contracts—his own and Miss Kitty's. Why? One of the producers had contacted Clay, the Colonel explained in answer to her questions. The film companies had reason to suspect that their payments ("thousands of pounds") had not been received by Mr. Fairfield, and, in addition, it was time to renew the contracts. Mr. Madrone would be calling . . .

Kitty held up her hand. "Wait!" she said in disbelief, feeling that she was viewing a movie and, although she longed to see the end, there was a need to back up the film in order for her to have a second look. "Do you mean they don't know of my father's death?"

"It would seem that they have no knowledge,

miss. Have you finished with your tea?"

Wordlessly, Kitty handed Colonel Witham her cup. Was there no end to this foul play? One layer of mystery surrounding her unfolded to reveal another layer—thicker and darker. Nothing was really resolved. The plot thickened daily.

". . . and so it is best that you not be alone. . ." The words from the gentle man startled Kitty. Such a short time ago it was Rhett who was mouthing the same phrases, telling her to be cautious—let him look after her—

"Are you all right, miss?" The Colonel's voice penetrated through the world of otherwhereness into which she was drifting again. "You look as if you had seen an apparition."

"I have, Colonel," Kitty said slowly, feeling the unreality of it all sinking in for the first time. "I have indeed seen a ghost—in the flesh—but I'm all right now."

The Colonel insisted on remaining to help "do the corners." Kitty knew that he felt his presence offered solace—security if not protection. And certainly he was good company.

Together they tackled the carpet. When it turned from brown to copper from their cleaning, the Colonel suggested doing the windows that Kitty had been unable to finish alone. As they worked, she voiced her bewilderment about the mortgage. The Colonel was as puzzled as she as to why her father had given him no hint, no papers which supported the transfer of the mortgage.

"But, of course," he said, "it is possible that Mr. Larry had no inkling that the men were scalawags. Or it could have happened—will you hand me the dry sponge, miss?—when Mr. Larry was too ill to be as alert as previously."

Kitty was beginning to believe that *anything* could have happened. She handed him the sponge.

"Thank you, miss. *Santhanas!*"

"What?"

" 'Get thee thence, Satan!' Your father is not here to say the words to the devil's helpers, so I shall be his mouthpiece!"

"Amen!" Kitty said.

•   •   •

Kitty ached all over after three days of bending, stretching, and "getting at the corners" with Colonel Witham. There had been no further disturbance and she was beginning to wonder if some of the incidents had been bad dreams. The house, except for the spare bedroom, was sparkling clean. And they would dig into the spare bedroom the next day, the Colonel promised. Kitty dreaded the task. It would be good to have him with her, and he seemed genuinely pleased that she agreed.

"The little house here reminds me a bit of some of those on the moors, you know. It has always been dear to me."

"Well, you've earned a share in it," she smiled, turning away. "The puppies are growing, aren't they?"

The Colonel agreed that the "small beasts" were indeed growing. Then, with a promise of seeing her the next day, he left. He was no more than out of earshot when the telephone rang.

Clayton! Her heart sang out. But it was the young man who had helped her at the bank. He introduced himself as "Mr. Thomason Alexander" and reminded her again that the bank was at her service. Then, clearing his throat importantly, he burst out with his astounding news.

"There was no opportunity to continue when you were here, but the computer furnished some additional information in its cross-referencing." He paused as if testing her interest.

"Yes?" Kitty prompted, wondering what it would be.

"We are a branch of the main bank in Tucson, you may know, and I followed through on the code number. We do try to be very thorough—"

"I appreciate that. Now, what has this to do with me?"

"Oh, I was coming to that. My superior is pleased that I checked," Mr. Thomason Alexander (or was it Alexander Thomason?) said with ill-concealed pride, "*and* with what I found! You see, the mortgage was paid in full from an account set aside in Mr. Fairfield's name by International Films, acknowledgment of which bears the signature of a Mr. Lester Teel. I assume that he has power of attorney?"

Paid in full . . . paid in full . . . the mortgage was paid in full. The phone slipped from Kitty's nerveless fingers. From some distant planet, the metallic voice of a man was saying, "Miss Fairfield—Miss Fairfield, are you there?"

As if in a dream, Kitty recovered the black instrument and spoke into it. "Yes," she said faintly, "I'm here. But I don't understand—"

"Oh, we understand, Miss Fairfield! No more snafu—situation normal, I assure you. If you and Mr. Teel can come in—Miss Fairfield?"

"I don't know a Mr. Teel—I will bring the Colonel—Colonel Conrad Witham—"

"Indeed, yes, I was coming to that. You see, there is," he cleared his throat, "a—well, sizable amount of money deposited in his name in Tucson. It appeared strange until our infallible system revealed—by cross-reference, you know—that this is separate and apart from your father's estate. It is our opinion that the beneficiary is unaware—the attorneys as well...duty to inform all involved...further business..."

Thomason Alexander, or whatever his name, went on talking. But Kitty heard no more. Eventually he stopped, she supposed, for the dial tone filled her ear. Then she hung up. She must pull herself together and get to the Colonel immediately. News like this would not keep.

The sun was dipping in the west. The hills were picking up the mysterious shades of purple that she loved. A walk—no, a *run*—would do her good! "I won't take the car—it's too slow!" She laughed foolishly and raced down the road.

Colonel Witham was unable to believe his ears. And later Kitty was to wonder if he really *had* danced around the room with her or if it was just another of the desert mirages! They would talk tomorrow, she promised. Never mind cleaning the spare bedroom. They must get to the bank. And now she must go. It would be getting dark. Then, still wildly happy, she skipped out the door, ignoring the Colonel's offer to walk her home. She did not hear him call, "Will they notify the law firm?"

It was dark when she reached home. Kitty started to let herself in, only to realize that in her haste she had forgotten the key. Then she must have left the door unlocked. With that thought she drew a breath of relief.

It was strange, she thought, as she turned the knob, that Jane Doe didn't bounce out to meet her. Strange, too, that the back door stood wide open. Hadn't it been closed? Well, she smiled remembering, it had been an exciting exit.

Jane Doe needed an outing. But the whine of the puppies said their mother had been gone long enough. Better whistle her in and lock up for the night. Kitty went to the open door and whistled softly. When the dog did not respond to the signal, Kitty knew there was a problem—but what? She was about to go out onto the now-dark patio in search when a sound caught her ear from inside. It was low and muffled and seemed to have come from the bedroom that she and the Colonel had not explored. Her first thought was of Jane Doe.

Unaware that she was tiptoeing, Kitty eased back into the living room and stood listening. If the dog was trapped inside, she would scratch on the door. Trapped? Hadn't the door been closed? She strained her ears for another sound. The wait was short. This time the sound was louder, as if something heavy were being moved from one spot to another. A crack of light showed beneath the door.

While she stood in the middle of the living room wondering what to do, the door to the spare bedroom began to open slowly. The clamor inside the room continued, telling Kitty that the latch of the door had not caught and the door was opening on its own. And then what she saw caused her to gasp aloud.

"Rhett!" Her cry was born of despair rather than fear. "Tell me what I'm seeing isn't true—all along I kept hoping—"

Instead of defending himself or soothing her with his usual cajoling words, Rhett turned the blinding beam of the flashlight into her face. As if hypnotized, Kitty stood statue-still. Watching the beam enlarge. Knowing that meant Rhett was advancing toward her. Yet she had lost a will of her own.

Even as he reached her, grasping her arms and pinning them to her sides, Kitty stood limp and lifeless. She could see Rhett's face fully now that he had left the dark bedroom.

His deep tan had vanished so that there was no longer a white rim near the hairline, and his lips looked thin and bloodless.

"It was you all along, wasn't it?" Kitty whispered when at last she was able to speak. "You took my purse—cut the fences—and came here, letting me see you—I don't understand." She shook her head back and forth, trying to clear it—trying to believe the horrible thing that was happening.

Rhett's nails cut into her arms, but she hardly felt the pain. The hurt inside was so much deeper. Tears filled her eyes and brokenly she continued, "It was you—it had to be—who sent the fake notice to Colonel Witham—broke into his house—" Kitty felt herself begin to tremble.

Rhett spoke for the first time, his voice scarcely recognizable in its raspy harshness. "That counterfeit nobleman! Nothing but a carpetbagging itinerant, sweet-talking his way in here, quoting obscure passages—and all the time keeping you here—"

Kitty felt the blood begin to flow back into her body. "This is my home, Rhett. Nobody talked me into staying. But that doesn't explain—let go, you are hurting my arms."

Rhett tightened his grip instead. "I didn't want this to happen. I really didn't. Even now, you can prevent it." He bent his head toward her frighteningly. "Where are the books? *All* of them. Don't you see, Kit-Cat," his voice dropped to resemble the tone he had once used, "that we can erase the past—that it can be just you and me, the way it's supposed to be? We can leave and start all over—we're tied together like I told you."

In a quick, surprising motion, he crushed her to him. The embrace was more frightening than his grip of fury had been.

"I don't know what you're talking about—"

"The ledgers—the ones Witham kept and the ones your father kept in secret—"

Kitty tried to pull herself free. "I can't breathe, Rhett. Let go so I can explain."

"You'll explain anyway!" His voice was harsh again. "We're not apt to be disturbed. I saw to that. Car's parked out back and that mongrel's put to sleep beside it and—"

"Jane Doe! You didn't—" Kitty gasped.

"Just a tranquilizer. The ledgers—*now!*"

"Even if I gave you the books, it would do no good. There are other records—and—oh, Rhett, this makes no sense! You have everything—so why, *why?*"

"Why?" Rhett's arms slid with lightning swiftness up her back and his hands were about her throat. "I never meant it to end like this—"

End! He'd said *end!* Rhett was threatening to kill

her! The room came into focus. And the God-given instinct for survival took over. She could not hope to win in a physical struggle. Words were her only weapon.

"Maybe you're right, Rhett," Kitty heard herself saying. "Maybe we *could* work something out—a business arrangement—" aware that the strong fingers around her throat had tightened, Kitty went on desperately, "or even something— well, more personal—yes, a *very* personal relationship—"

"I'm not sure I can trust you. I'd only planned to scare you, get you off my property—"

"Your property?" Kitty knew then that Rhett's violent behavior had nothing to do with the outdated mortgages and the forged signatures. "What claim do you have?"

"Does the name Teel mean anything to you?"

Teel? Gwendolyn Teel on the envelopes addressed to her father . . . Lester Teel had signed for payments never recorded . . .

"I am Lester Teel—your stepbrother." *Stepbrother!* The room swam crazily. It made sense and yet it made no sense at all. "Why?" Kitty whispered again. "Why do you hate me—even if what you tell me is true?"

The powerful fingers formed an iron band around her throat. "I don't hate you, Kit!" The words came out pitiously.

For a moment she thought he was weakening, reconsidering whatever dreadful thing he had in mind. Then a crazed look came into his eyes. He was a man obsessed. "It's your father I hate! And what he did to my mother. All these years I have waited until just the right moment, laying plans carefully to take what should have been hers. I grew up in poverty—without enough to eat. She was forced to work in cheap dives and finally go out in the streets—"

Nobody is forced to do that, Kitty longed to whisper. But he was beyond the point of reasoning. Aloud she said, "I'm so sorry, Rhett—Lester. So sorry. I—I didn't know. And neither did my father, I'm sure—"

"He knew!" The words came out in a frenzied scream of fury. "And now you've spoiled everything—"

Totally out of control, he babbled on and on. Mechanically Kitty asked leading questions as a delaying tactic, praying all the while. *Hold me up, Lord. . .give me strength. . .put the words in my mouth. . .until You can get help to me!*

Time lost its meaning as the man she had known as Rhett Dawson confessed that the Gotschalk father and son knew nothing of the situation— "just a bumbling old man and his idiot son, a pair of trusting fools." His fingers still clutched her throat, but the grip had not tightened. Kitty grew faint but stood absolutely still. Sometime during the dreadful ordeal she heard a weird, unearthly howl. At the sound, Lester Teel's fingers closed in.

"Sleep!" he said. "Dying's better than living as I have. . ."

17

It was a very strange dream—vague and fragmented, the way of all dreams, but still strange. Somebody had broken into her house...Jane Doe, growling as Kitty had never before heard a dog growl, had shredded the legs of the intruder's trousers and was working on the sleeve of his plaid shirt. A man who reminded her of the Colonel was standing apart from the scene with a shining object in his hand. "Don't move!" he was saying in clipped English—"not even a muscle, or I shall be compelled to blow a hole through you, sir!"

Kitty wanted to laugh, but there seemed to be no breath left in her lungs. Perhaps she'd laughed too long already . . . oh, it was funny—so funny that she had crumpled to the floor. And there she lay as the dream went on . . .

Two men in uniforms came . . . police, they told her, one feeling her pulse, the other telling her not to be afraid . . . and then they were handcuffing the intruder, whose face looked familiar. If only her eyes would focus properly as she was lifted up . . . .

Voices she recognized at the time but would be unable to identify later (or was it the other way around?) ran together: "Oh, the dastardly fellow, a regular poltroon, took the back road . . . yes, Miss Fairfield entered the house alone, unprotected because he had maliciously done in the poor beast . . . but, revived, the animal alerted me to danger. . . . If Miss Fairfield will be willing to testify (another voice) . . . oh, yes, Captain, Miss Kitty will indeed . . . the whereabouts of Mr. Clayton Madrone (third voice) . . . yes . . . and may I add that the miss here was a heroine in her own right, stalling as she did until the beast could howl out the S.O.S.

The telephone shrilled and the Colonel (yes, that had to be his voice) answered. "Oh, yes, I assure you, Mr. Madrone, everything's under control! It's always the butler, you know."

That was the funniest line of all—a fitting climax to the comedy. Kitty tried to applaud, to laugh, to speak. But she drifted into the kind of blackness in which there are no dreams.

● ● ●

When she awoke, Kitty's mind was surprisingly clear. The Colonel was trying to force broth into her mouth and she kept pushing it away. There were a million questions to ask. But the one she voiced was, "When will Clay be home?"

"Tomorrow, miss. Open your mouth."

Kitty longed to put the ill-fated evening and the dreadful events leading up to it behind her. But that was impossible, for too much that lay ahead was strung into it. And so she sipped broth and drank tea prepared by the Colonel as the two of them went over each detail and made plans to tie up all the loose ends when Clay came home. Hours slipped past unclocked.

"He'll be proud of you, miss. You handled the crisis jolly well, you know. He has the contracts for your signature as well as the royalties—"

"Royalties?" Kitty almost choked on the lamb chop that Colonel Witham had decided she could have the evening before Clayton's return.

"Yes, miss, International Films shares in the profits in accordance with the arrangements made by your father and the senior Mr. Madrone."

So that is how Clay manages to support his radio ministry, was Kitty's first thought. And then came her second reaction: "I must have a little money—"

The Colonel nodded. "Now, you must rest."

But Kitty was unable to sleep. She was safe now— no problem there. The house was hers. She could support herself. And she had proven to herself that she could cope—maybe even manage alone. "But I'm not a loner, Lord," she whispered. "I guess You didn't shape my heart for that. How can I make Clay see?"

The Lord hadn't let her down so far. He wouldn't start now. And with that sweet thought in mind, Kitty drifted off to sleep. In her dream it was tomorrow. And Clay was holding out his arms— so warm, so strong, so protective. She rushed into them with a cry of joy. "Oh, my darling," she whispered, "why fight what you want so much?"

When she awoke, the world was pink with dawn. Had the dream been an answer telling her to be bold? She trembled at the thought. "Today is the day!" she said over and over, nuzzling the puppies, then hurrying to the shower. "He's coming home!"

As Kitty emerged from the shower, her freshly shampooed hair dripping little rivulets down her face, there was a knock at the front door and a bark of excitement from Jane Doe. Wrapping a terry robe about her quickly, Kitty ran barefoot into the living room and released the lock, expecting to see the Colonel.

A tall, lean figure stood silhouetted against the now-rosy horizon. Clay! A Clay she had not seen before—dressed in dark trousers, an open-throated white knit sport shirt, and a casual summer jacket. But it was something else that caused her to gasp. His beard was gone.

"Hello, Kitten Eyes," he said.

His beloved soft, deep voice stirred her almost more than she could bear. Why then did all the words she had planned die on her lips?

"Kitten?" he said again. Kitty realized then that she had neither spoken nor invited him in. Still staring at the ruggedly handsome profile which the beard had covered, she motioned him inside. It was a new face—in a different sense—of the man she loved.

"Clay," Kitty managed to say, hoping her voice sounded normal, "I'm just surprised to see you so early—and with a new face."

"Same old face," he shrugged. "I brought these for your signature—and thought we should get an early start. The Colonel will be ready by the time you're dressed. I'll feed you in town."

Wanting to cry, Kitty accepted the papers with trembling hands. She had hoped for a joyous reunion—the kind in her dreams. He should be telling her how brave she was, how he realized now that he couldn't live without her. Instead, he was matter-of-factly laying out a blueprint for her day without so much as a "by your leave." The disappointment made her tense. And so the two of them stood: Cool. Polite. Formal. A million miles apart.

As if sensing that an intervention was in order, Jane Doe bounced from her box and began whining and licking Clayton's hand in invitation. She had waited long enough to show off her litter. "Sorry, old girl!" He leaned down over the puppies and began stroking their soft little bodies. "Get dried off," he said to Kitty, "and we'll be on our way to wind up all this business—pretty babies, Jane Doe!— in about 15 minutes. Okay?"

"No, it isn't okay! I can't be ready—"

"Fifteen minutes," he said in a peremptory tone. He rose to his feet and, taking her shoulders, turned her around and propelled her toward the bathroom. For one rebellious moment she hesitated. What right did he have being so autocratic, treating her like a stick of furniture he owned? Then the moment was shattered by his voice: "Or can't you manage alone?"

Quickly she dived into the bathroom and turned on the blow dryer. Annoyed as she was, Kitty had to laugh when she caught a look at herself in the mirror. Would she ever, *ever* be at her best when he saw her?

In exactly 15 minutes he knocked on the door. Kitty surprised him by emerging with her hair pinned becomingly on top of her head and wearing a white wrap-around skirt and a cool, green-sprigged blouse. He was about to speak, but Kitty turned toward the door. Shortly afterward the three of them were on their way to the pueblo.

• • •

In the days that followed, Kitty seldom saw Clayton alone. There was so much more to attend to than she had realized. They were forever with a banker, a lawyer, or a member of the cast for the next movie (who needed to consult with them regarding availability of certain buildings and props). Too, the Colonel was with them on their frequent trips into the village and the two trips to Tucson. It was natural that all talk would be directed to settling all the affairs of the "Circle Left," the inheritances, and the motion picture contracts. As grateful as she was for the assistance, Kitty felt frazzled—and a little resentful. There had been no more mention of her working with Clayton—something she had looked forward to—and there was a growing feeling of a widening gap between them. She longed to close it, but had no idea how to.

In the little spare time she had, Kitty read through all the books she had brought home to better prepare herself for helping when the time came. She continued listening to Clay's morning meditations, wondering when he found time and energy to prepare them. Her first impression was that he kept hoot-owl time. She knew now what a dedicated man he was.

The season wore on. The creamy-white blossoms of the saguaro gave way to purple, apple-shaped fruit—the kind Clay liked for jelly. Kitty wished for time to gather the fruit, get the recipe from Mrs. Donohue, and surprise him. It would be a way of saying "Thank you." But her schedule grew even busier. The puppies were beginning to explore the house and required training. Feeling that danger was past, Kitty began to go through the boxes her father had packed.

First she read through the heartbreaking letters her father had written and never mailed to her mother. Always they ended with, "Say the word, my darling, say the word and I'll come for you." But her mother, so carefully coached by her own mother in woman's passivity, had never found courage to say the word.

It was in the midst of her reading that a sudden insight came to Kitty. It was so real and so clear that she wondered how she could have missed it. "Why," she said aloud as she let the letters flutter to the floor, "our pasts are as parallel as the wires between power poles! The four of us have let our pasts shape our lives and keep us from happiness: you, Clay, Rhett, and myself! We've been living out our parents' failures, fears, and hates—instead of the love they should have had!"

Tearfully she picked up the letters and retied them. Some day she would read the rest, but only after she had made certain that the three of them still living were released from the past. It was then that Kitty knew for certain that she would be unable to press charges against Lester Teel. He would be held accountable for the financial ruin he had heaped on others as well as herself. And he would be punished even more inside. But, even living out his mother's shoddy life as he had tried to do, Kitty felt that he would have come to his senses in time. Accused by her, however, his intentions would probably be interpreted as attempted murder. *No*, she decided.

The decision was comforting. Kitty looked at the bundle of letters in his mother's handwriting, feeling no temptation to read them. They belonged to the past. Let her son dispose of them in due time. . . .

And so the days tumbled end-on-end. Kitty had reached the last trunk when she found what she knew immediately to be *The Dress*. It meant something special or her father would never have folded it away with such care. She removed the last layer of tissue and gasped with delight at the fiesta dress— a long, loosely flowing, blue-flowered skirt and an ivory satin blouse.

And then she saw the tiny envelope pinned to the sash. Inside she found the first—the only— message of love she had ever seen or heard from her mother. The note was unsigned, but the handwriting was unmistakable. "Through the years— with you!" The words on the urn. Their signal of love.

"Oh, Mother!" she sobbed. "I wish I had known

. . . we could have talked . . . found a way for love . . ."

Kitty was sobbing so hard that she failed to respond to the commotion in the living room. Some part of her knew that there were a million barks, a door that slammed, and maybe a chair overturned. But she was too spent to care.

And so she was totally unprepared for a pair of gentle—then not-so-gentle—arms that lifted her to her feet. "Kitten Eyes, my darling, what's happened? Oh, Kitten, stop crying—you're breaking my heart—" Clay's voice wavered.

Kitty snuggled against his smooth-shaven chin and reveled in the glory of being close to him. Then, a little wildly, she pulled back and gave way to a new flood of tears.

Clay was dumbfounded. "I—I—Is *that* how I've been treating *you*—oh, Kitten—*please*—you've been through so much—"

But Kitty went on crying. "It's not that . . . it's that you never told me I was doing well . . . never let me help with your work like you promised," she choked, "and these letters showing the wasted years . . . and we're doing it, too . . ."

Clay was smoothing back her hair, kissing her forehead, and then wiping her face with a handkerchief as big as a bedsheet. "Get that thing off my face!" Kitty all but screamed. "You're trying to smother words you don't want to hear—just like you smother your feelings. You tell us not to be afraid," Kitty's voice rose and she made no effort to lower it. "And you—*you* are the biggest coward of us all! You are afraid to love—you don't dare!"

With a deep breath, Clay put her away from him. Kitty was too spent to care. She had made a fool of herself, but at least she had not made her mother's mistake of silence. She had offered herself to the man she loved, and been turned down—rejected.

"You don't understand—you don't understand at all—" Clay was running his hand through his hair.

"Your mother, and Colette?" Wearily Kitty turned her eyes to his face and was surprised to see that he did not wince. "I understand it all—also that all other women are shut out, including me—the wayfaring stranger you took in like the horned toad."

"Lizard. And now if you will stop behaving like a woman scorned, let me tell you that I did have some things to sort out, in all due fairness. And, although I was attracted to you from the beginning, I had to make sure for your sake I was freed—"

"God freed us. You said so!"

"Ouch! You are right—right about everything. And don't think it was easy keeping my fine resolutions!"

"Bah—"

Clay ignored the interruption. "Then, while I was away, I came out of hiding. I hoped that shaving the beard off would give you some inkling."

"Showing your face is not showing your heart."

"You're not giving me much help, you know. Aren't women supposed to be supportive?" Clay attempted a grin.

"I, too, have emerged."

"So I noticed." Clay's fingers were busy with his hair again. His face was white with strain. "That'o another of the problems," he said slowly. "I wanted you to find who you were, to be sure what you wanted—and there was a time when I wondered if Rhett meant something to you. Now," he grasped her hands when she would have interrupted, "hear me out. I found out differently in a hurry—but I felt you needed a recovery time after finding his real identity. How *do* you feel, Kitten?" His voice was low.

"He is my stepbrother, but he is a stranger. And yet," her voice broke then, "it hurts in a way I can't explain."

Clay drew her palms to his face and held them there. "I understand. And I want you to know that I've arranged for him to have psychological help until there is an indictment—"

Kitty could feel the pulses throbbing in his temples. She longed to throw her arms around his neck and kiss him in gratitude. But her heart could never stand another rejection.

Kitty swallowed and nodded. "Thank you," she mumbled.

Still holding her hands to his face, Clay said in a deceptively calm voice, "Will you marry me?"

Marry! The word hung between them. Kitty's astonishment was beyond measuring. "Why?" she finally managed.

"*Why?* Why do other people get married? Because they're in love!"

"You never said you loved me."

"I do!" He gripped her wrists, bringing her palms hard against his cheeks, pursing his lips temptingly. But not yet! Kitty forced her head back.

"I never said I loved *you.*"

"But you do—oh, darling, you do! I've known all along—"

Kitty pulled away completely, feeling her eyes enlarge with emotion. "There you go, telling me how I feel...taking over my life...expecting me to live with your weather-pattern moods. You'll make a terrible husband!"

"I know."

"You're bossy, unpredictable—and *wonderful!*"

Who reached out first? What difference did it make? Their arms were wrapped around each other. Everything was perfect. And then she burst into tears.

"Oh, Clay—I'm a mess—I look awful, *awful*—"

Clay let out an exaggerated sigh. "Then fly to the bathroom—or shall I escort you—?"

Kitty flew.

● ● ●

The wedding was simple. The Colonel and Mrs. Donohue stood up with Clay and Kitty, hovering over them with such dedication that Clay said afterward he was afraid the witnesses would say the vows for the bride and groom. The minister of the little village church officiated, his words intoning in the empty building like an echo from the past.

And in a way it was. Kitty wore the quaintly beautiful blouse and skirt she had found in the trunk, knowing beyond all doubt that it was her mother's wedding gown. The sash, she found, emphasized her tiny waist, and the scooped neckline of the satin blouse allowed the right space for the ribboned cameo necklace which was to have been a gift from her father. The finishing touch was the dainty cameo earrings.

And her ring, like the giant bouquet of sweetheart roses, was a gift from the groom. It had belonged to Clay's mother...so beautiful...a circle of diamonds around a flashing emerald...left behind... like her love...

But they were here, the parents that Kitty and Clay loved—and had forgiven. There was no other audience.

Kitty, her eyes ablaze like the emerald she wore, took her vows demurely. But when Clay kissed her, it was hard to restrain herself. She longed to... *well, why not?* Boldly she tossed her bouquet to an astonished Mrs. Donohue and threw her arms about Clay's neck. "I'm supposed to submit to my husband," she whispered.